[Type here]

STAY OR GO?

BY KAREN JONES

Stay or Go?

Printed in the United States of America

First printing 2023

Prologue

If God existed, he gave her more than she could bear.

Was that a Bible verse? It no longer mattered. Her empty mind and soulless heart contained no capacity to process it. Sarah thought nothing, felt nothing, and sensed nothing on the hike. In the past, trekking here filled her cup and lifted her eyes to the rocky cathedrals. This mountain cirque was her church, connecting her with the energy of all. Now the earth-anchoring tether snapped. Sarah did not know where else to come. She simply could not endure anymore.

A group of determined trees hid a second glacial lake. Ignoring them, Sarah sat on a flat granite rock near the shore. She pulled a half-empty water bottle from her pack. The warm water washed the dust out of her mouth and trickled down her shirt. Not noticing, she reached into the bag again. Something slipped out more substantial; weightier. Sarah grasped its ergonomic grip and pulled out the gun. Mike's gun. He taught her how to use it before Mia entered their lives.

"You have to know how to protect yourself."

Mike taught her about shooting. At the time, Sarah couldn't imagine a single circumstance when the weapon would be needed. But the unimaginable can happen. The owner of a gun shop was happy to provide lessons in exchange for the purchase of ammunition. Now she knew.

Baby Steps

Sarah chanced upon Mike her senior year of nursing school. He hung around the periphery of the campus in hopes of attracting coeds, especially party-loving nursing students. Mike revved the engine, and the vibration of the motor sent a tingle through Sarah. The shiny chrome of the Harley accentuated his laughing gray eyes. Add the sexy scruffy beard and the whole picture made her hot.

"Hey I'm Mike," he grinned. "Wanna ride?" As Jerry Maguire had Dorothy at "Hello," Mike had her at "Wanna ride?" The single ride extended to afternoon jaunts, which extended to weekend excursions. Sarah's life was intermixed by studying for nursing school and then riding wild with Mike on the Harley. On their happiest weekend trips, they scooted to little rural towns in Montana. They checked into the town's only motel. As soon as the motel door closed, Mike grabbed her shoulders sliding his hands over her breasts.

"Get over here girl," rasped Mike. Sarah nodded eagerly. Sex was fearsome for quiet Sarah. Mike's dominance sent electrical charges from her nipples to her nether parts. It took a while, but she learned to ride Mike's wave of passion to find her own pleasure. He kissed her head as she lay in the crook of his arm and felt loved. Sarah looked back on these first years feeling unfettered and deeply in love with the free-spirited man. Mike knew how to play. Sarah's too-serious side was thrilled at being invited along for the trip.

Sarah started a nursing job in a rural hospital after graduation. They moved into a boilerplate apartment. Mike worked at a motorcycle repair shop. Actually, many repair shops. They came and went with the seasons. Closed because of no business. Closed because the partner buddies argued. Mike's instability caused fights but, in the end, Sarah's steady income evened out Mike's sporadic pay.

Mike needed health insurance, so they married with a Justice of the Peace, Sarah repressed the longing to create an intimate family wedding with her mother. Baby Sarah's surprise conception late in her parents' lives produced a loving family for a single child, but both had passed. Fortune smiled when Mike signed on with a Harley shop. A job in a large garage not a buddy's shop. Good pay and benefits. The best yet, Mike loved the work. He often came home late but smiling. Kissing her deeply, he tickled her face with his beard. They ate a late meal laughing over stories of the customers and fellow employees of the shop. Mike and Sarah enjoyed their lives. Work was meaningful. They loved their weekend motorcycle trips. Money earned interest in their savings account. Sarah felt a yearning for the next step in their lives.

Sarah approached Mike during a weekend away, after their lovemaking. She lay on her side walking her fingers to his mustache.

"Mike, I think it is time."

"Time for what?" he asked drowsily.

"To start our family." Sarah felt Mike's body tense next to her.

"Now? You want a baby now?"

"We finally have everything we need. My job, your job, money in the bank. I love you so much Mike, I want us to be a family." She looked into his eyes trying to detect his thoughts. He caught her look in time and shuttered them.

"I don't know. Things are so good now. I don't want to run off the road.

"Run off the road? What does that mean? We planned to have children one day. Remember you wanted two and I wanted five?" She grinned at him, lightening the mood. "I tried to compromise at three, but you said no way so I said I would have twins the third time around." The corner of Mike's mouth rose a little at the memory.

"Please, let's talk about this seriously." Mike expressed doubts, but in the end, he caught Sarah's enthusiasm and capitulated.

"Never mind my crazy fears. OK, let's make that little baby." Sarah should have asked what changed his mind. She didn't want to know; she wanted a baby.
Sarah fantasized, about a more intimate kind of lovemaking. More tender. Soul binding. Soft touches and murmurings. But Mike wanted the usual fare of naughty boy/naughty girl sex. Conceiving a baby felt wrong this way. She tried to tell Mike, but he laughed swatting, her on her bottom. "Come here, you dirty girl. Daddy's got a present for you." She felt robbed of such a meaningful time in her life. A husband and a wife lovingly making a baby. What other options were there? She wanted a baby and obviously needed Mike's cooperation. Mike was not going to cooperate unless they played the usual sex games.

One afternoon at the nurse's station, she rose suddenly to retrieve a chart. Unfamiliar nausea ensued. *I'm pregnant.* Racing home at the end of the shift, she peed on one of the ten packages of pregnancy tests she bought months ago. First one — positive! The second one — positive! The third test might be overdoing it, but it revealed the same happy news. *Mike!* She waited outside until Mike rumbled into the driveway. He pulled to a sudden stop when he saw her.

"We're pregnant!" Sarah shouted.

Mike hesitated a moment before he said, "That's great! We are going to be parents." Mike laughed at her joy, hopped out of the

7

truck, and swooshed her in one big hug. Fatherhood had arrived, for better or for worse.

Sarah experienced significant nausea in the first trimester. Mike rushed home to do chores as he watched her pale face with its greenish tinge. That ended with the arrival of her second trimester. Happy energy filled its place. She jumped out of bed, took a shower, and cooked Mike a huge breakfast. He sleepily walked into the kitchen. Preparing the food just a few days ago before would have sent her right into the bathroom.

"What's this all about?"

"I'm better," she grinned, flipping a pancake in the air. Mike did not complain as he dug into the breakfast worthy of a king.

Her joyful second trimester exceeded her pregnancy expectations. Co-workers exclaimed at her glow. Her energy abounded. Her libido roared back, much to Mike's pleasure. Sarah didn't care what kind of sex, as long as they were having sex.

They decided not to find out if the bender of the baby until it's birth. Her friends at work tried to get her to change her mind.

Sarah's best friend Jane complained petulantly, "How am I going to buy the right color baby clothes?" Jane was Sarah's closest friend. Sarah smiled and shook her head.

"Fine, I'll buy a clown suit to cover every possibility."

Stay or Go?

Her growing baby bump provided another thrill. She took lots of sideways selfies showing the weekly growth. Sarah loved maternity clothes that hugged instead of hid the baby bump, buying too many, rationalizing they would use them again in another year or two.

One afternoon at work, Sarah did not feel well. Her back hurt but she attributed it to the overweight patient in room 10. After hauling another patient out of bed, a hot trickle ran between her legs. Sarah rushed to the bathroom. Peering into her panties, she saw blood--a lot of blood. Running downstairs to the obstetrical ward, the doctor examined her. By then the backache progressed to cramps. Sarah called Mike, and he sped to the hospital in time for the ultrasound.

The doctor admitted Sarah to the hospital. He prescribed medications to stop the labor. With the tests complete, he talked to them. "Your results are normal. You do not have high blood pressure. The placenta is intact. Your cervix is firm. About 25% of the time, we don't know why premature labor starts. I think this is the case with you."

"Will she," Mike caught his breath. "Will she lose the baby? Will Sarah be all right?"

I think we will be able to keep on top of this. I'll give you some prescriptions to take at home. You will have to stay on strict bed rest."

"How long?"

"Until the baby is born, hopefully at term."

During the last seven weeks of pregnancy, Sarah endured interminable worry mixed with unending boredom. She watched reality tv until it turned her mind into jello. Baby books were memorized. Lots of naps. Mike prepared meals which they ate playing card games at night. She enjoyed the closeness and fun during these games.

Jane helped the most. She brought the best medicine of all - laughter. "I almost amputated a finger of a lady last night."

"What?"

"She was on a ventilator and couldn't talk. She would tap her wedding ring on the bed rail to get my attention. I didn't mind at first, at least she could communicate. But the steady tap-tap-tap made me crazy after a few hours. I went to our normal plan B, which is to tape the wedding ring. So it wouldn't get lost, I told her. Somehow, she managed to thump her taped ring as loud as the damn metal ring. Thump-thump-thump all night long. At about four in the morning, Alicia found me rummaging through a surgical kit for a scalpel. They had to restrain me in a wheelchair. Of course, they pushed the chair right next to Thumper!"

Sarah laughed at the obviously exaggerated story. She looked forward to Jane's frequent visits, friendship, and the good medicine of laughter.

Sarah's water broke at 37 weeks.

"This is it!" Mike carried Sarah's hospital bag and drove to the hospital. "Are you sure you don't want to take the Harley?" he joked. Sarah didn't answer as her first deep contractions started.

Sarah had written a simple birth plan – labor naturally, if possible, then go for the epidural. She experienced enough deliveries from work. Natural birth women bearing excruciating pain, moaning, groaning then ultimately screaming the baby out horrified her. She had a hidden terror about childbirth and planned to depend on modern medicine. Her birth plan was executed perfectly. After 3 hours of labor without anesthetic, 4 hours with an epidural, and one hour of pushing, the doctor exclaimed the magic words, "It's a girl!" Sarah was thrilled. She fell wholly and completely in love. So did Mike, by the look of joy on his face. They agreed on the name Mia. Beloved. Mia entered their lives.

Sarah's heart beat high in her chest on discharge day. The proud parents dressed Mia in pink, with Mike's sizable fingers struggling with the small snaps. A slight panic arose when they thought the car seat was not installed correctly. Mike drove slowly, Sarah sat with Mia. Then everybody home and baby makes three.

Sarah panicked when maternity leave ended in eight weeks. Nobody could take care of Mia like she could. The thought of being away from Mia for a day was unbearable. But finances dictated returning to work full time. Sarah found a daycare months before Mia's birth. The daycare maintained an excellent if not expensive reputation. Sarah took to the owner immediately. Still, Sarah gripped the car seat with white knuckles entering the daycare. The owner said with a voice of kindness, "What a beautiful girl. We are so lucky to have her." A few tears spilled over Sarah's eyelids, but she let go of the car seat and drove to work.

A baby changes everything, and Mia proved no different. Mia fussed, especially at night. Sleep deprivation prevailed. Working, pumping breast milk, dropping off, picking up Mia, fixing dinner, and maintaining the house exhausted Sarah. Mike stepped up with a bit more effort. As soon as he got home, he strode directly to Mia's crib, swooped her up, and played with her. His efforts never counterbalanced the full load. To be fair to Mike, Sarah thought that only she knew how to care for Mia. Mike was pushed to the sidelines.

Life progressed, the first three months a total haze, the second three calmer. Mike, Sarah, and Mia built their family. Sarah celebrated her love for Mia by decorating her neck with an intricate calligraphy tattoo of the letter M, filled with interwoven pink wild roses.

With warmer weather, Mike grumbled about getting back onto his motorcycle. Once he put Mia in front of him on the bike and inched it down the street. It didn't last long. He brought Mia back screaming. Even with hearing protection, the loud muffler and the vibration proved too much. That ended that. Sarah smiled inwardly. Babies and Harleys don't mix.

Between breastfeeding and paying the expensive babysitter, the couple could not resume their weekend trips. Sometimes Sarah would shoo Mike away on her weekends at home so that he could clear the cobwebs from his head. Sarah enjoyed the one-on-one time with Mia. She loved walking through the zoo in her stroller. Mia, covered with a hat, waved her sunscreen-lotioned arms at the sun. Though too young to understand, Sarah sat with Mia telling her the names of all the animals, imitating their sounds. By day's end, Mia would be sound asleep in the stroller. Sarah felt her love for Mia bursting out of her heart.

Mike enjoyed little outings too, at first. He would preen when women commented on "such a pretty baby." But to be honest, he was capable of only so many walks in the park.

"If you don't like what we are doing, you can find a family activity for us."

First, he wanted to attend a tailgate party with his friends. Good idea, but bad timing. The weather turned stormy, so Sarah had to stay in the truck with an increasingly fussy little girl. Sarah signaled Mike several times to leave, but he turned his back, taking another swig of beer. Next, he thought it would be fun to drive up to the town where his buddies planned a rendezvous. Another idea dashed by an ear infection.

Mike wanted to ride his bike every weekend. Fights slipped into their routine. Mike's face looked perpetually grim. This baby stuff cramped his dreams. Sarah felt some fabric of their marriage stretched, but as soon she gave serious thought to it, Mia cried for attention.

Every mother thinks their child is the brightest and most beautiful child on the earth. If a mother doesn't feel that, whoever will? Mia's hair grew into soft blond curls. Her hazel eyes peeked out from behind plump cheeks in a perpetual state of smiles and laughter. Mia's sense of humor permeated her personality.

"Mama look!" as Mia somersaulted across the room in her t-shirt and shorts. She stood- "ta-dah". Sarah applauded as one who has seen a Cirque du Soleil.

Mia heard the rumble of Mike's truck and waited by the door. He opened his arms and Mia scrambled onto his shoulders.

"Up Daddy, up," she commanded. Who could resist her appetite for play? Mike bounced up and down.

"Vroom, Vroom, let's kick into high gear. Hold onto the handlebars, we are going for a ride." They played their favorite game - Mia riding Mike the Harley. She squealed with happiness. Mike careened around the room, pretending to crash into a low arched ceiling. He stopped suddenly, and Mia's body leaned backward in response.

"Again!" Mike trotted around the room, giving Mia the bumpiest ride possible. "Bumpy road, bumpy road," sang Mia.

"Enough," groaned Mike. As one last hurrah, he pretended to drop her to the floor. Mia's infectious bright smile bonded the family in laughter.

Sarah fixed a half-hearted dinner. Her hospital staffed minimally regardless of patient census. Lots of patients with little staff today. Frozen fish, rice, and frozen vegetables graced the table. Nothing to write home about.

But not For Mia. Her diet consisted exclusively of two things. SpaghettiOs and meatballs in a small thermos for day care. Boxed macaroni and cheese for dinner. Sarah tucked fish and vegetables on her plate. At the end of dinner, Sarah triumphed with a few bites of ingested fish. Every morsel of greens remained on the plate. Mia eyed her mother sideways seeing if she noticed the vegetables in plain sight. Sarah sighed, thinking at bedtime a banana or a fruit cup of mangoes would provide better fare.

Dinner invigorated Mia, "Mommy, will you play with me?" That sounds like an innocent question, but it had conditions. Playing with Mia means giving her 1000% of your concentration. If your eye drifted to a television news story, Mia pounced immediately.

"Mommy, will you play with me? Will you play with me?" By this time of night, Mia had dressed as a Disney princess from her costume box. Most likely she arrived with stuffed animals for imaginary play. Mom was assigned Teratops. Mia performed with Blue Bunny.

"I hungry for hay, "said Blue Bunny." Teratops placed hay on the ground and Blue Bunny chomped it up.

"Sleep time," signaled that all were to lay on their sides and snore honk-shoo, honk- shoo.

"Blue Bunny hurt leg." Teratops trotted over and kissed the leg. The adventures continued from flying, to crossing rivers, then finding magic sprinkles. On other nights Mia charged out from her room dressed as Cinderella brandishing a large plastic saber.

"I kill Zombie." She found imaginary zombies in each room of the house, successfully slaying them.

Sarah had been taught to sew by her mother, and she loved making frilly dresses for Mia. As often as not, she found the dress on the floor, and Mia dressed in a princess costume.

Mia's ballet dancing endeared Sarah the most.

"Dance today, Mommy?"

"No sweetheart five more days until class."

Mia missed nothing that her dance teacher taught her. She overflowed as preciousness in her pink leotard, tutu, and slippers. Of course, Mia wore a costume tiara each week, not part of the required dress.

Sarah exhibited little grace. Clumsy was the blunt description. It amazed her when Mia straightened and lifted her carriage with each plie and releve. She turned gracefully in a circle, ending exactly at her beginning point.

Mother and daughter shared a special closeness during the bedtime routine. Mike watched tv, and Sarah preferred he didn't intrude on this time. First, a bath, Mia being very particular about how hot or cold. "Is it hot hot Mommy?"

"No."

"Is it cold, cold Mommy?"

"No, it's just right Mia." Mia swished the water with her hand and was satisfied. Mia gathered a large bucket of bath toys and dumped them in the tub. An old Barbie past her prime served as Mia's scuba diver. Of the multitudinous bathtub toys, Mia favored a wind-up submarine that made its way to the side of the tub bumping against the porcelain.

Sarah leaned back on the toilet, closing her eyes to let relaxation seep up her back. Her job required quick thinking, mental as well as inhuman strength. She listened to Mia play and talk to her toys. After twenty minutes Sarah washed her child's curls and soft skin. Mia clambered out of the tub into a soft white towel. Sarah gently rubbed her dry. Off to bed.

Of course, they had the ritual storybook. Tonight, they read a favorite: But Not the Hippopotamus. Mia chimed in "But YES the hippopotamus" in the end, being satisfied that equality ruled the world.

Sarah sat on the side of the bed, this time for a mother and daughter duet.

"Hush little baby don't say a, here Sarah stopped, and Mia chimed in — wurd,

Momma's going to buy you a mocking - - burd.

If that mockingbird won't - - *sing.*

Momma's gonna buy you a diamond - - *wing.*

If that diamond ring turns --*brass,*

Momma's gonna buy you a looking- -*glass.*

If that looking glass gets, --*brokt.*

Mama's gonna buy you a billy - - *goat.*

If that billy goat won't - - *puull,*

Momma's gonna buy you a great big- -*buull.*

If that great big bull knocks you - - *down,*

You'll be the sweetest little baby in town.

Sarah sang the last line while kissing sleepy Mia on the forehead. One more sacred ritual they recited together:

No scary monsters in this house.

No bad dreams in this house.

No silly spiders in this house.

Mia fell asleep in minutes. Sarah would watch her sleep, wondering as her translucent eyelids twitched a dream. What will Mia be like when she grows up? What will she do? There will be professions that have not been invented. How many children? -- Sarah's grandchildren? A passel of children like Sarah wanted. As the months passed by, Sarah saw this possibility fade.

Mike called one night. "I'll be home a little late; there's a job I need to finish. Will you two be OK?"

"Sure, a little overtime always helps." Mike came home in time to kiss Mia's soft head. He came home late a few more times. Once, Sarah smelled beer on his breath.

"You've been drinking."

"Oh, the guys and I went out for a beer after we finished the job." Sarah didn't care he had a beer; she felt surprised Mike didn't tell her. And maybe a little bit hurt he didn't come home directly to them.

At the end of the month, Sarah paid the bills. She anticipated the extra money from Mike's overtime to pay down the pediatrician bill. No extra money appeared on the check. Squinting at Mike's pay stub, she saw only forty hours each week. "How much overtime did you get last week?"

"Oh, I don't know, I didn't keep track of it."

"Did Payroll forget? There are only 40 hours on the stub.

"They must have forgotten. I'll talk to them tomorrow."

When Mike came home the next day, Sarah asked. "Did you find out about the missing overtime?"

"Yep, they forgot to add it in. I will get it next payday."

But the next check was short, again. Sarah brought the pay stub to Mike, "Do you mind telling me what is going on? No overtime, again?" Silence. "Mike?"

"OK, I just – I needed - I couldn't tell you. I go out for a beer with the guys. I need to let off some steam after work before I come home. I get home and everybody jumps all over me. A guy doesn't have a chance to rest his boots. I relax an hour with the guys; then I am ready to be the family man."

"You can't come home to let off steam? You lied to me! I counted on the extra money. The strain of their marriage weighed heavier on her shoulders.

The next week Sarah plopped on the sofa next to Mike. "She's asleep."

"Huh? Oh good," admiring his new arm chain tattoo. "I need a babysitter for the weekend," said Mike nonchalantly. "Brett and some of the guys want to ride to Winchester. Remember how much fun we had there?"

"You know I have to work this weekend."

"Duh, why do you think I wanted you to get a babysitter?"

"By the time we pay for a babysitter all weekend I might as well not work -it costs too much."

"I am sick and tired of babysitting every other weekend when you work!"

Stay or Go?

"What?" stammered Sarah, shocked at the vehemence of his words.

"You have changed. You used to love to ride the bike and would drop everything for a weekend trip."

"Yes, I've changed since we met. I changed when we had Mia!" she shouted. This tactic covered familiar ground in their tenuous marriage. This time the fight flamed higher.

"I am stuck here every other weekend babysitting Mia."

"Since when do fathers babysit their children? You can't babysit your own daughter." Mike's eyes narrowed. Sarah continued. "Do I ever babysit Mia?" her voice strident.

"Mommy, tv is so noisy," a small voice peeped from the bedroom.

They stood both glaring; their bodies angled away from each other, and Sarah whispered harshly. "You can play with your child, laugh with her, buy her McDonald's, watch her sleep, see her play...." Sarah saw Mike's eyes glaze over, but didn't care. She stormed on, ".....teach her colors, sing a silly song, go to the zoo with her." Sarah couldn't help but sound shrill. "But you cannot babysit your own daughter!"

"Goddamn it, I have to get out of this house, away from you, and yes, ------ a break from Mia. I'm leaving Friday night. I'll come home Sunday."

"If you are so keen on going, why don't you head on out now."

"Fine." Mike stomped upstairs and stuffed his clothes in his athletic bag and hurried out the door. "I'll see you Sunday; then we are going to have a do-or-die talk." The words didn't frighten her. She was ready for a Come to Jesus meeting too.

The Come to Jesus meeting came. Not Sunday, but Saturday night. Sarah woke to her cell phone chiming. She groggily thought something had happened at the hospital. She answered with a sleepy hello, then heard Mike's slurred voice.

"You gotta come get me."

She sat, instantly awake. "Mike?"

"I'm in jail in Winchester. You gotta get me out."

"Jail, wha-- what happened? Are you alright?"

"I'm fine. That damn bitch cut me off, and I skidded off the road. Fucking cop didn't give a shit. He wrote me a goddamn book of tickets and hauled me here."

"Why are you in jail for an accident?"

"Cop said I stunk like alcohol. I wasn't goddamn drunk; I told him. He asked me to take one of those breathing tests. I told him to go fuck himself. He cuffed me so tight I still can't feel my hands. Sarah, you gotta get me out of here. Go to the ATM and withdraw $500 for my bail."

Sarah froze into complete silence.

"Sarah! Get the hell down here,"

"I - I can't. I have Mia, Mia's asleep."

"Just bring her and get me out of here."

"I am not getting Mia up in the middle of the night. You can damn well stay in that filthy jail until I decide I am good and ready to come to get you." She hung up furious. In the morning, with Mia settled in daycare, Sarah drove to retrieve Mike. There were papers to be filled out and bail to be paid until a sober and sullen Mike was released to her care. They drove the two-hour ride home in complete silence. At home, Mike started towards the bedroom. "Mike! Sit down. We have a lot to talk about."

"Jesus Christ Sarah, I didn't get one minute's sleep in that crap hole which is YOUR fault because you refused to bail me out." An ugly fight escalated. Mike denied being drunk. He asserted he drank two beers at the bar. The lady cut him off, and he swerved into the ditch. Once his buddies saw he wasn't injured, they called 911. The gang drove off in a rush.

"You should have taken the Breathalyzer" she seethed.

"I wasn't drunk."

"Now you are automatically guilty of a DUI. If you took the damn thing maybe it would prove you weren't drunk." Though she …. doubted it.

The next day she made Mike call the attorney's office. "Are you kidding me? How much? Are you out of your mind?"

Mike reported, "Pretty much $6000 for the lawyer. A whole slew of fines on top of it all. Both lawyers say it will probably total close to seven or eight grand before it is all done."

"That is more than our savings."

"I got a couple of guns I can sell. That will bring us maybe $1000."

"We have to sell the Harley."

Mike stared her down. "Don't even go there. The rest we will put on the credit card."

"We don't have that much credit."

"I guess I better get some." Which he did, at astronomical interest rates.

When Mike left for work on Monday, Sarah protested. "Your license is suspended, you can't drive. The insurance is canceled.

"We have to have money. I'll drive carefully."

Sarah's stomach clenched. She was tired of *we's* when it came to financial obligations. The worst we came when Mike got the quote for new insurance. It increased the premiums by more than $6000 a year.

"We can't afford these premiums."

"We'll drop the insurance."

"You know we can't do that. We still have loans out on the cars."

"I don't have to insure the bike."

"We still can't afford the insurance."

"I'll take care of it." He bought a policy at the only high-risk insurance company in the state. Sarah had no idea how to make those monthly payments.

They stopped speaking except for critical communication about Mia. Despite Sarah's efforts to be cheerful around Mia, the toddler instinctively felt the tension, becoming cranky. Her three-year-old temper tantrums increased.

Coming home from work a month later, Sarah found Mike sitting on the sofa. Fifty more pounds added to her overburdened shoulders. The news would be bad.

"Got laid off. "

"Some jerk squealed that I lost my driver's license. I need one to test-drive the repairs."

"That isn't getting laid off, that is getting fired!" Sarah shot at him. Mia put a finger in her mouth, arched her head back, and started to cry.

If things had been cold between Mike and Sarah since the DUI, it turned into a frozen winter landscape now. Mike looked for jobs repairing motorcycles, but with no driver's license, he came up empty-handed.

The Harley Dealer protested Mike's firing, denying him unemployment insurance. The financial burden of the DUI suffocated Sarah. Mike watched tv or puttered with his bike while Sarah called creditors asking for new payment plans. Everybody offered a new arrangement, at a monthly amount well above their nonexistent budget.

"Mike, you make these calls and figure out which bills we can pay. I prefer to keep a house with electricity. He made a few phone calls and shuffled through the stack of bills. He swept everything off the desk and then stewed in front of the tv. The mess overwhelmed Mike, his anger surged.

Sarah kept Mia in daycare full-time, to maintain their slot if Mike got a job. Sarah hung up with their mortgage company. Things looked grim. "You have to get a job."

"I've looked everywhere."

"I know there aren't any bike shop jobs, but you have to find something, anything. We are going to lose the house."

"What do you want me to do, work the night shift at 7/11?"

"Yes, if that is what it takes to bring income into the house. If you can't get a job, then you are going to have to sell the Harley."

 "I am NEVER going to sell the Harley."

Sarah pressed on. "I looked online. We could make five or six thousand dollars. It won't pay off your DUI, but it may save our house."

"This is what you wanted. All this time you wanted me to sell the bike. Goddamn it, I'm not going to do it. The bike is the only thing that is mine in this house and I am not going to sell it. This is all your fault you know."

" My fault?"

"You knew good and well I didn't want you to get pregnant. You got what you wanted and now you get to live with it."

Mike had never been this cruel before. It seemed like Mike punched her once-pregnant belly.

"Get out." her voice low. "Get out now."

"Really? I get to leave this prison? This, this," he swept his arm around the toy-strewn floor," is way more than I signed on for. I am happy to get out from you and the bills and the fights and," he almost said, Mia, but bit off the word. Mike jammed his clothes into his athletic bag.

Sarah couldn't sit so she found a bag, stuffing it full of things from the living room. She threw the bags in the garage, hitting the bike. "Take your shit, your bike, and get out. "

He did.

As the next weeks went by, Sarah expected to hear Mike in the driveway to see Mia. She found herself tuned for the familiar rumble.

Mia asked day after day, "When Daddy come?"

"He went on a bike trip with his friends. Daddy will be home soon, sweetie."

Mia no longer bought the story after a couple of weeks. "When Daddy coming mommy, when?" Sarah had to admit to Mia, "I don't know honey." Mia wailed. "I want daddy." It hit especially hard when Mia cried out during their special bedtime ritual.

No monsters in this house.

No bad dreams in this house.

No silly spiders in this house.

Daddy comes home, Mia added.

Sarah's heart broke completely.

Mike never did come back. He never called. The lawyer could not serve the divorce papers which asked for a meager $350 a month in child support, and papers transferring all of Mike's DUI debt into his name. Since the car and the truck were registered in both of their names, the insurance rates couldn't be lowered.

Mike vanished. Sarah's pride prevented her from calling his buddies. She called his mother, who distractedly said, "Why no honey, we haven't seen him."

Work, bills, Mia. No family to help. The cold reality of single parenting. How much more could she bear?

THE LOVE THAT WAS MIA

Sarah struggled through oil-thick air for the next two months. She had to keep working. The bills reached astronomical proportions. Mike's truck couldn't be sold without his signature.

Mia now needed extra daycare every other weekend. It mortified her, but bankruptcy loomed. The lawyer charged a shocking amount of money to file suit. How ironic, she thought that you pay such a large amount to a lawyer when you have the least amount of money.

Sarah surrendered the keys to the house to the bank. They moved to a small apartment close to daycare. It was pretty run down, but everything worked. Sarah slept on the sofa. The neighborhood could be safer. Every penny was pinched until it bled.

Exhaustion overwhelmed her every waking moment. After dinner, she tried to participate in playtime while lying on the sofa. Of course, Mia detected her less than 1000% attention and peppered her with "Play with me Mommy, play with me, Mommy." The iPad distracted Mia for short periods. Even then, she bored quickly.

"Mommy, play with me," jumping next to Sarah. Mia brought her stuffed toys over so Sarah could play on the sofa.

"Blue Bunny is sad." Mia acted so convincingly that Sarah had to look if this was play-acting or real. "She doesn't have any friends."

Sarah trotted Teratrops over to kiss Blue Bunny. "I'll be your friend."

After a few weeks, Mia grew less interested in active play. Crawling on the sofa next to Sarah, they watched cartoons. Sometimes Mia fell asleep before bedtime.

One evening, Sarah undressed Mia for her bath. There were almost ten bruises on her little body. Mostly on her arms and legs, but two on her torso. "Mia – how did you get these bruises?"

"Owies?" she asked.

"Did you hurt yourself?"

Mia shook her head, hair flaring around her face.

Sarah tucked it in the back of her mind to ask the daycare if she had been in any rough play. It slipped into her mind fog. She remembered at work but then forgot about it.

A few days later, Sarah cooked dinner while Mia watched cartoons.

"Mommy!" Mia shrieked in a way Sarah knew signaled a real emergency. She ran out to the living room.

"My God!" Mia's mouth dripped with blood.

"What happened?" The toddler continued to scream. Sarah ran for a cloth. She wiped the blood as it streamed from Mia's nose. Scrambling in the kitchen, she put ice in a baggy and then applied pressure on the child's face. When the bleeding clotted to a trickle, Sarah swooped Mia in her arms and sped to the hospital.

The ER admitted Mia immediately. Sarah tried to keep the child from panicking with a quiet voice, distractions, songs, anything. The blood draw challenged them the most. Mia remembered shots from her immunization and liked them no more than any three-year-old. It took skilled staff to draw the necessary blood. Her nosebleed started again when she screamed.

Sarah waited for the pediatrician to arrive, rocking Mia in her arms. Surprisingly, Mia slept.

"Dr. Roberts!" She jumped when he entered the room.

"Sarah." He held the lab reports and scooted the stool closer. "There is no easy way to say this. It looks like Mia has a serious blood disorder. It may be leukemia." He touched her shoulder. "I'm so sorry." Sarah's oil-thickened air congealed.

"Leukemia? How do you know for sure?" Sarah said, panic rising in her voice.

"I don't know for sure, of course. Mia's white count is sky-high, over 100,000, and full of immature cells. Her platelets are very low, causing the nosebleed."

Sarah thought about the bruises a few weeks ago, and felt overwhelming guilt for not taking Mia in for a physical. Meanwhile, Dr. Roberts conducted his exam, noting more physical symptoms. "Her face is pale. Has she been tired lately?"

Sarah told him about the naps on the sofa, plus the early bedtimes.

The doctor drew a card out of his pocket. "This is for Dr. Patel, the top oncology hematologist at Children's Hospital in Salt Lake City. I called, and they will give Mia direct admission.

"Sarah," he said gently, "We have to transport Mia there now. Her entire immune system has collapsed; she needs immediate care."

"Today! Oh God, I should have caught this sooner! Mia had all the symptoms, but I didn't take it seriously."

"Her leukemia started months ago. You could not have prevented it. The ambulance arrives in an hour. We will insert an IV to start antibiotics. Go home and pack everything you need. Mia will be hospitalized for at least six weeks."

"That long?"

"That's the average first course of chemotherapy. Dr. Patel will further diagnose Mia, make a treatment plan, and explain it to you further. Her mind flooded with details of what to pack. Payday was yesterday, so she had the money for gas. She could not afford a hotel. As if reading her mind, the doctor said, "They will let you sleep on a folding bed in her room."

Work, what about work?

Sarah called Jane with the shocking news.

"I'll tell the supervisor. Don't worry about anything. How can I help? What can I do for you?"

"I have no idea," Jane promised to call Sarah the next day.

Tears ran down her face as she prepared for the long stay. She threw clothes haphazardly into a bag. She returned to the hospital just as the ambulance loaded Mia, now with the IV line.

Stay or Go?

"Mommy!"

"Sweetie I am going to drive our car right behind you to the new hospital. I promise I will be right there."

"No Mommy I want to go with you," sobbed Mia.

The skilled paramedics quickly established rapport with their young patient. Mia clutched a long-haired stuffed bunny, while the woman made the bunny "talk". Sarah saw Mia smile. They closed the back doors and the parade of two vehicles drove to Salt Lake City.

Children's Hospital's recent renovation welcomed children. The exterior was painted and lit, so the rectangular angles of the building looked like colorful blocks. Gigantic neon animals decorated random sections.

The paramedics rolled Mia into the ER as Sarah drove to the parking garage, and dashed up the stairs. Mia had perked up considerably. "Look Mommy, a zoo!" Mia exclaimed as she looked at the jungle animals painted in bright colors on the walls. Good to Dr. Robert's word, the cheerful ER admission clerk typed in a few strokes, finding Mia's name.

"We are expecting you, she said. Sarah held Mia while answering the woman's questions. The ambulance crew packed the stretcher and equipment.

"Bye-bye Mia!" Mia waved her hand. "Did you thank them for the bunny?" "Thank you, Miss Jeannie."

The clerk smiled at Mia. "Do you want to walk to your room, have Mommy carry you, or do you want to ride in the wagon?" A brightly colored wagon sporting Disney princesses sat in the hall.

Well, that's a no-brainer

Mia's eyes grew wide, happiness flowing over her face. "Wagon! I ride wagon!"

"What a great treat," enthused Sarah. "You can be Princess Cinderella in her carriage."

"Our kids get to ride in wagons all of the time," said the desk clerk.

Sarah balanced the heaviest of the travel bags on the back of the wagon. The serpentine path to the room confused her. If they left her alone, she would never find her way back to the front door.

The clerk cheerfully oriented her. "Here's the cafeteria, it is open 6 AM to 8 PM, The food is stocked with snacks after normal hours. The play area is there. All the children participate in play therapy as an important part of their care. Over there is the adolescent quad. Teens are admitted together there. Sometimes they come to the younger children's ward to read stories or play games. It benefits both. Around the corner are the teacher's offices so that kids can keep up in school.

They passed a children's ward. Eight beds occupied the cheerful room. The kids seemed to be from ages five to almost ten. Some of the children rested in bed receiving IV's. Some played in a well-supplied toy area. Sarah could not help but notice there was not one piece of hair to be seen on the children, not one. "Here's Mia's room."

Sarah picked up Mia as they entered the private room. A single hospital bed occupied the room with solid bed rails on all sides. A television hung on the wall. There looked to be a DVD player and a video game remote. A comfortable-looking chair sat to the side. A window seat was covered with a long thick cushion. The hospital parking lot made for a depressing view.

The admitting nurse arrived. Her scrubs sported Finding Nemo patterns. "Hi! I'm Michelle," she smiled, and introduced herself first to Mia.

Mia ducked her head into Sarah's shoulder. Shy toddlers were nothing new to the nurse. She started by orienting them to the room. "Does Mia sleep in a bed or a crib at home?"

"A bed. Mostly my bed. I am going through a divorce; it has been unsettling for her."

"Are you going to sleep here?"

"I don't want to leave Mia."

"You can shower in the bathroom; there are linens to make up the folding bed. Here at Children's, we have a strict policy that children cannot sleep with their parents. Even if they are careful, a parent can accidentally roll on the child or any tubes."

"I don't see Mia cooperating."

"We tell parents to carry out their bedtime ritual and put their children to bed. If they cry, every five minutes you can briefly comfort the child, then lay them back down. Keep it non-emotional. The kids get the hang of it quickly. They are often tired from treatments, so they sleep quite a bit." Sarah was dubious.

Michelle brought in three different hospital gowns gaily printed with pink teddy bears, Superman or Pretty Ponies.

Another no-brainer.

The nurse helped Mia dress as a Pretty Pony. She still clutched the rabbit, so changing clothes involved passing the stuffed animal arm to arm while protecting the IV. "I like when the ambulance crew gives the children a clean stuffed animal. Toys from home can be pretty grungy."

Michelle explained the procedure for washing her hands when entering or leaving the room. She taught the rest of the infection control procedures. "Now when the rest of the family comes —"

Sarah interrupted. "There is no other family. It is just us, "Right Mia?"

"Sometimes Daddy." Sarah winced, giving an imperceptible shake of her head.

The lab technician drew blood from Mia's arm. Sarah thought that her child would need a transfusion after taking so much blood. Mia cried out, but the specialized staff completed the procedures from a child's perspective. "When Mia gets her central line, we will be able to draw the blood from the line instead of poking her."

As Sarah digested this, Dr. Patel entered the room. She was a handsome woman with smooth brown skin. Her shiny straight black hair was shoulder length. The white lab coat indicated her status. She smiled, introducing herself. "Dr. Roberts talked to me. I understand we have an urgent situation. The first thing we need is a differential diagnosis to determine what type of blood disorder Mia has. If it is leukemia as the preliminary findings suggest, we need to see the extent of leukemia in her body."

"I didn't know it could be in anywhere other than her blood."

"Leukemia can most commonly spread to the bone marrow, the spleen, the liver, the spinal fluid, and even the brain. We will complete quite a few tests. I will need an in-depth look at her blood work. A bone marrow aspiration is needed so we can examine the cells. A spinal tap is required to look for leukemia cells in the fluid. Finally, there will be an MRI to see if leukemia has affected the brain."

Sarah could not imagine Mia suffering through these invasive procedures. "I don't know how she will do it."

"We give different types of sedation based on the procedure. Preventing pain is one of our top priorities. Mia will need a central catheter. We will have enough test results back that we can start her chemotherapy the next day."

"So quickly?"

Dr. Patel proceeded to give Mia a thorough physical exam, all the while taking an oral history from Sarah. The procedure finished, Dr. Patel said kindly, "I know this is overwhelming. We have social workers available for you. The nursing staff is quite compassionate."

"What are Mia's chances of….recovering?"

"I'll have more accurate answer for you when I get the test results back." Sarah despaired. What happened in a few short months that she lost a husband, and a home and ended up here at Children's Hospital?

"Don't forget you have me to talk to." Dr. Patel considered Sarah's eyes with kindness. She felt fortified, with a bit more strength.

Sarah's prediction of Mia's refusal to stay in her bed was born out. Mia looked tired, and frightened, wanting nothing more than the comfort of her mother's body. Sarah tried to establish the nighttime routine of a story, their son, their anthem. Tucking Mia in bed lasted less than five minutes before Mia stood and rattled the bed rails. Sarah followed the nurse's instructions. After many tears and total exhaustion, Mia finally slept in the bed.

The next morning the nurses sedated Mia for the central line and MRI. Sarah marveled at the decorated department which looked like an aquarium. The MRI table looked as if it was drifting into a fish cave. Mia slept through the procedure as planned. She remained sleepy while enduring the spinal tap. The bone marrow aspiration required a bit more sedation.

Back in the room, Sarah flopped in the chair, barely keeping her eyes open. What a relief that Mia still slept. The nurse hung another dose of antibiotics. They followed with a bag of fresh frozen plasma, adding more platelets to Mia's blood.

Sarah knew Mia needed to understand her disease. The admission packet held a helpful information sheet. With Mia fully awake, she settled in Sarah's lap.

"Mia, you know what blood is. It is when you get an owie on your knee and red comes out. The red stuff is your blood. The doctor says your blood is sick." Mia looked tentative. "We are going to stay in the hospital for a while. The nurses like Michelle give you medicine so that your blood won't be sick anymore."

"Will medicine be icky?"

"Most won't be icky, but some might be a little bit icky."

"Did I make my blood sick?"

"No honey, you didn't make your blood sick. It got sick all by itself."

"Will you stay with me, mommy?"

"I will stay with you. Sometimes you will go with the nurses, but I will wait for you right here."

"Don't want to go!" wailed Mia.

"Mommy will always be waiting right here, with, uh, Bunny!"

Mia put a finger in her mouth, but calmed down, hiccupping. "Daddy see sick blood?" Mia said with growing anxiety. "Daddy sleep here? Daddy find me?"

That twisted a knife in Sarah's gut. Where the hell was Mike - Mia desperately needed him. Sarah felt torn in two. One part of her screamed, slashing her fingernails down his cheek for abandoning them. Another part yearned for Mike to be a family again, to share this burden.

"I don't know sweetie." How could she comfort her fatherless child?

Sarah reflected as Mia slept. Their midnight ritual could be called an anthem. A song from which only good will come. A recitation to keep trouble away. A plea for what is wanted. Sarah had no religion, considering herself an agnostic. She believed in the interconnectedness of all people, animals, the earth - everything. The Golden Rule covered all situations.

Sarah lost her Christian beliefs one day in front of the television. A newly released film documented the liberation of a concentration camp. The view of the skeletal prisoners, the stacks of stiff dead people, the disease, and the living conditions overwhelmed her spirit. The British made the S.S. soldiers bury the dead in a pit half the size of a football field.

An epiphany descended into her soul that night. Certainly, these 10 million people got on their knees to pray with every fiber of their souls to be saved from this hell. They prayed that their missing families would be safe. They pleaded to God that he would take their lives so they would not suffer so. They prayed that their children be spared from pain. What kind of God would refuse the prayers of such suffering? The similarities of other genocides arose in her memory. Every person had prayed to the depth of their soul, and God didn't listen. After this, she could not pray. How could one meaningless prayer stack against the prayers of the prisoners of the Holocaust? It could not.

When Sarah discussed this with friends, there seemed to be two responses. It is God's will. Or, it is not for us to know God's plans. Sarah could only think that if it was God's will to let 10 million people suffer and die then that is not a God. That would be evil itself.

Now Sarah sat in the chair contemplating her sleeping angel. What if God did exist? What if she read the whole situation wrong? What if a plan existed for Mia and the other children on the ward? What if praying would keep them alive? Sarah slipped off the chair onto her knees leaning on Mia's bed. Sarah prayed with every fiber of her soul that Mia would live. Just to cover her bases.

Sarah waited for the doctor. Mia's sedatives wore off, and she awoke happy. The children's iPad occupied her all morning.

"No need to enforce screen time here," bemused Sarah.

Breakfast went well. "Hungry Mommy."

"Do you want eggs?" Mia nodded her head.

"Do you want cereal?" Mia smiled.

"What else?"

"Peaches, Mia asserted.

Lunch had its challenges. "I want SpaghettiOs," declared Mia.

"Honey, they don't have SpaghettiOs's" that set out a howl of indignation.

Sarah admitted to the dietitian about Mia's penchant for processed foods. Her meal trays contained a balance of nutrition, plus hidden protein packed in the pudding or the chocolate shake. Mia picked through the food, but not enough to meet her new nutritional needs.

Right after Sarah placed the scantly eaten tray by the door, Dr. Patel came in and sat on the window seat. She patted the cushion for Sarah to sit. "We have most of the tests in," stating in her slight Indian accent. "Mia has acute lymphoblastic leukemia or ALL. It is the most common type of childhood leukemias."

Sarah nodded, the information identical to her research.

"We have a standard chemotherapy protocol. But we have a few," she hesitated, complications. First, her white cell count is unusually high at 102,000. We don't like to see a new patient with their white cell count over 50,000."

"So, what does that mean?"

"There is one other thing. Mia has leukemia cells in her spinal fluid. This means that the leukemia has spread. We have diagnosed her as high-risk ALL."

Stay or Go?

Sarah felt nauseous.

We will add another drug to her chemotherapy cocktail. Unfortunately for Mia, the side effects are harsher. We will start her on steroids to help with that. As you may know, steroids have their own set of side effects."

"I read that ALL usually has a 90 - 95% cure rate. What do these complications mean now?"

"That means we will start the chemotherapy and see how Mia responds."

Sarah asked many questions. Dr. Patel carefully answered them all. Again, she examined Mia into a laughing fit before leaving.

"Mommy sad."

Sarah quickly faced Mia pasting the happiest smile she owned on her face. "Oh no Mia." The doctor is going to make your blood better. We will go home then."

"Daddy be there?"

"Do you want to play with me?" Sarah distracted her.

Day one of chemo passed without problems. Sarah and Mia played with Play-doh. A Pretty Pony grew spaghetti hair when the molded head was compressed. After the thrill of the hair had passed, Mia shaped the dough.

Stay or Go?

"What's this mommy?"

"A bird?"

"No! A kitty."

"What's this mommy?"

"A dog?"

"No! A fish.

Sarah never guessed correctly.

Day Two began the nightmare of complications.

"Mommy?" Mia's voice woke Sarah, who reached for her child.

"I sick." And she was, all over herself and the bed. Sarah pushed the call button for the nurse. The nurse administered a powerful anti-emetic, but Mia continued to vomit. Sarah held the plastic emesis bag. Mia grew hot and sticky. Sarah placed her on her side, gently patting cool, wet clothes on her forehead. Michelle hung a new IV bottle to prevent dehydration.

"I sick."

"I know you are honey."

"When will I be better?"

"Soon, honey."

A few days later Mia developed a sore on her lip. She cried when Sarah tried to put Vaseline on it. A nurse came. "Mia, sing a silly song with me. It goes "Ah!!!" Michelle quickly peered into her mouth. "There are a couple of ulcers there, too. Remember chemotherapy affects the gastrointestinal system the worst. The mouth sores are part of that."

An ointment applied to the outside sore helped a bit. Mia needed another medication to swish and swallow, but her nausea made dosing difficult. Diarrhea emerged soon after. Her bottom was inflamed in an angry red despite soothing creams. Sarah placed diapers on her potty-trained child.

Sarah nursed Mia with what felt like a terrible flu. Mia listened while Sarah sang the bedtime song, but only joined in the finale in a whisper.

No monsters in this house

No bad dreams in this house.

No silly spiders in this house

Daddy find me.

A problem arose when Michelle came to change the dressing on Mia's central catheter. It hadn't occurred to Sarah that Mia saw it as a huge sticky band-aid. Mia screamed, "No, no, no!"

Stay or Go?

The nurse said, "Children are often fearful of the dressing change."

Sarah convinced Michelle to let her take the dressing off. She knew how to maintain sterility and remove it at a pace Mia would tolerate. It took 45 minutes to ease the sticky dressing off, but Mia kept calm. Mia's blond hair fell out quickly, Sarah bought feminine pink and purple headbands from the gift shop. As often or not, Mia preferred tiaras. The side effects continued unabated. Mia's sparkling eyes dulled. The steroids swelled Mia's face. Dr. Patel came in one morning to examine her. "I think it is time for a feeding tube. Mia is not able to eat enough calories. I would like to put a tube through her nose into the duodenum. The tube feedings will perk her up quickly."

Sarah consented, maintaining the same attitude for this new tube as for the central venous catheter. The tube would bring life and wellness to Mia. The doctor placed the feeding tube, taping it to Mia's face.

Dr. Patel proved right. Within two days Mia snuggled with Sarah and watched cartoon movies. They sang together.

"Old MacDonald had a farm," sang Sarah.

"E-I-E-I-O," refrained Mia, careful of her mouth sores.

The recreational therapist came. Mia instantly fell in love with him. Why not? He had an infinite variety of toys and gave Mia his 1000% attention. Sometimes they played with Mia's choice of toys. She favored Pretty Ponies. Sometimes a therapeutic bear stood ready for medical procedures. Mia injected the bear with enthusiasm.

Days passed slowly. They settled into the hospital routine. Mia's fatigue increased. Lots more naps. Her recreational therapy slowed. Sarah sat next to Mia stroking her face. She lightly touched her back and tummy until Mia's skin rose in little goosebumps. Nurses drew blood from the central line. Mia endured a spinal tap every week. There were surprising times when she woke energy and happiness.

"Mommy color with me?" The hospital supplied rainbow markers with coloring books. They colored contentedly. She tired easily, laying back without finishing her picture, and falling asleep.

At the end of week two, Sarah's anxiety about the new blood and spinal tap results ran high. Many children went into remission now. Dr. Patel's news crushed her hope.

"Mia still has leukemia cells in her spinal fluid. There are fewer cells, but of course, there is no acceptable level. I am going to adjust her chemotherapy protocol a bit. Let us see what another week brings." Later that week, Dr. Patel came wearing a mask. "The chemotherapy has damaged Mia's blood cells so that her neutrophil count is dangerously low. We will have to stop treatment for a few days."

"Will the leukemia start growing again?"

"Anytime we stop the chemotherapy, is a time we are not treating leukemia. Hopefully, her blood count will rise in a couple of days, and we can start again." Reducing the chemotherapy did ease Mia's nausea. She ate a little ice cream and a little pudding.

"What kind of ice cream do you want, sweetie?"

"Banilla." Though the feeding tube provided her primary nutrition, Mia enjoyed the sensation of her favorite foods in her mouth.

At night, on her knees, Sarah made a special point to God about Mia's blood count. Sarah despaired and made an appointment with the social worker. Arriving, she sat on the comfortable sofa and cried. "What is happening? Mia isn't getting any better."

"Do you have any family who can come be with you?"

Sarah shook her head.

"So, you are carrying this burden alone?" the social worker asked gently.

Sarah nodded.

"Do you have a faith that sustains you?"

Sarah thought of the hours on her knees by Mia's bed. "Do I have faith that sustains m?" she said bitterly. "What kind of faith are you supposed to have if a God lets your child be desperately ill?" The social worker backed off that tactic, letting Sarah cry and rail as she needed to.

Sara walked down the hall. The mother of the boy next door approached. A huge smile filled her face and tears ran down her cheeks. "We're so blessed. Jeremy is in remission!" Sarah tried to lift her cheeks into a smile. "I am so glad for you."

"Oh, praise God that he has answered our prayers."

Sarah walked back to the room. For a heartbeat, she didn't recognize her child. Bald, moon cheeks, sunken eyes. Her anger mounted at a God who chose a little boy over her Mia.

Mia struggled to sit. "Why won't Daddy come?"

Sarah sighed. Mia deserved the truth. "Daddy was unhappy sweetie."

Mia frowned. "Mad at me?"

Sarah shook her head. "Mad at you?"

"A little. Daddy felt very unhappy. Inside of his heart." She pressed Mia's hand against her little heart.

"Where's Daddy?"

"I don't know. He went somewhere to feel better.

Mia's eyes welled with tears but didn't cry.

"I hope Daddy found happy."

That night's prayer ended differently.

No monsters in this house.

No silly spiders in this house.

No bad dreams in this house.

Daddy happy in his house.

Mia found her closure and asked for him no more.

Sarah and Dr. Patel waited together for Mia's laboratory results. Dr. Patel's warmth invited Sarah to tell stories about Mia.

"I think one of my favorites happened six months ago. Mike brought home this clown mask. It slipped over her head, so it looked like white clown paint for a head. There were glasses and a tremendous pickle nose. Mia is quite the performer. She wore the mask to her bedroom adding her Sleeping Beauty dress-up clothes. She debuted her costume and entertained us all night. Mia performed her ballet recital dance with perfect precision, all the whole hamming up the farce of the costume. What an actor. I laughed so hard my stomach hurt. God, how did we get from that laughing family to here?"

Michelle brought the reports with her eyes lowered. Dr. Patel carefully read the reports. She pursed her lips. "Mia still has leukemia cells. It seems this chemo protocol is not working."

"What now?"

"It is time to do a bone marrow transplant. We will use chemo and full body radiation to kill her blood cells. Then we will replace them with bone marrow that has stem cells. The stem cells will grow into healthy cells. Does Mia have any siblings?"

"No."

"A sibling would give us a 25% chance of a match. A parent would give about 1 in 200 match. If you do not match Mia's tissue type, we will apply to a donor bank for an exact match. Sarah's hands turned cold. She recognized their position as a turning point. Her child's life could tip either way.

The harsh treatment sickened Mia to the extreme. Mia no longer had the strength to play. Strict isolation procedures ensued. Sarah wore a mask, gown, and gloves. The mask needed changing hourly. The measures protected Mia from infection, but also erected a physical wall.

Mia awoke to a mother who only had eyes. Skin-to-skin contact was impossible. Sarah felt clueless about soothing her child through a mask and gloves. How many hours had she rubbed her back and massaged her forehead when Mia had a headache. She could still do these things now but behind the wall of thick rubber.

Mia spoke little. "Mommy I sick."

Dr. Patel came one afternoon. "We found a perfect match! It gives Mia the best chance of achieving remission." Sarah and the doctor hugged. For the first time, her chest felt light.

"Mia! We found a medicine that is going to make you better!"
Her beloved child smiled and struggled to sit. Sarah embraced
her, not even trying to hold back the tears.

"Mommy crying.

"Because I am so happy."

"Like Daddy?"

"Yes, like Daddy."

The rug was pulled out from under them before the celebration
stopped. The evening nurse took Mia's temperature,
compressing her lips. "Her temperature is 102."

"But she doesn't look any sicker."

"Bone marrow kids don't show many symptoms because we
have killed the cells that react to an infection." "Dr. Patel rushed
in around 10:00. "Mia has an infection that must be treated
immediately. I want to transfer her to the ICU to start
Vancomycin. "There will be no bone marrow transplant until
she is infection free." Sarah blanched. The antibiotic's toxic
properties hurt adults. How could Mia's little body manage it?
Sarah noted another tube, this time for oxygen. Her positive
attitude crashed. The medical staff rushed Mia to the ICU, with
Sarah close behind.

Mia's condition quickly deteriorated. She lay barely conscious. A
giant machine capable of handling many drugs replaced the
single IV pump. Another tube was inserted into her bladder to
measure urine. It seemed every few hours a new medication

augmented the other drugs on the complicated IV pump. Mia's heart weakened.

Over three days, Mia progressed from a nasal cannula of oxygen to a mask. Finally, her weak body struggled for every breath. Sarah agreed to allow a breathing tube and respirator for Mia's now comatose body.

At three in the morning. Sarah contemplated Mia's situation. One: A deadly infection raged in her sick little body. Two: She cannot get the bone marrow transplant unless she is well. Three: she ticked off, she is so weak she cannot take a breath on her own. Four: she is receiving a toxic antibiotic. Five: her blood pressure is so low that medications can't help anymore. Six: she is unconscious. Her nurse's training pronounced the facts. Sarah stayed on her knees and prayed with every fiber of her soul.

When the sun rose, Dr. Patel entered, this time with tears in her eyes. "Mia's organs are failing. We would have to start her on kidney dialysis today, but I do not recommend it. She cannot tolerate the Vancomycin. Sarah, I'm sorry there is no more we can do. Sarah felt the fracture of her heart and soul. Mia's wracked body hovered around death. Sarah rose from her cramped and calloused knees refusing to pray to a God who would not answer her prayer to keep her child alive.

"I'm ready. But I want all the tubes taken out. I want to hold her privately."

Mia left at the age of three years, six months, and two days. She didn't say goodbye. That was for the movies. A child actor on their dying day opens their eyes and says, "Mama. It's OK, I'm going to live with the angels."

Sarah left the room. The nurses removed everything, bathing Mia as they worked. They removed the breathing tube last.

Then Sarah held Mia, her beloved. She cuddled her intimately as if returning Mia to her womb. She sang their song with a pause as if Mia's spirit filled in the words.

No monsters in this house, promising Mia the safety of a new home. *No bad dreams in this house,* promising a happy afterlife. *No silly spiders in this house. Mommy will see you soon in your new house.* She rocked her baby for a long time, long after Mia had passed.

That night Sarah walked out to the car, alone, without her child in her arms, blocking out the shock and grief.

She called Mike's parents first. She bluntly told them, "I don't have money for the funeral."

"Don"t worry honey, we will take care of that. After the funeral, they slipped an envelope to her that covered the cost of the funeral plus more. Sarah tried to protest, but Jeanette cut her off.

"If you ever hear from Mike…"

"Of course, of course. We know Mike loved Mia, despite what he has done.

Sarah called Jane next. "Jane, Mia is dead."

Jane burst into tear." Oh my God, how can that be?"

"The chemo didn't work, she got an infection and died. One day we were coloring, then she was gone. I can't understand...

"What can I do?"

"Could you please call Johnsons' funeral home and ask them about arranging the funeral?"

"Of course." I know you are not all right, so what else can I do?"

"Could you take care of the whole funeral thing?" "I——-she paused, tits flowing again, "I just can't."

They held the funeral three days later, giving time for Jeanette and Glen to travel. Sarah struggled with the location. It seemed the only option was related to God and Christianity. Sarah thought conducting it in Ma's bedroom would best express the loss. She would be crazy trying to carry out that plan. Sarah chose the small chapel room. Jeanette, Glen, and her work friends filled it with delicate bouquets, appropriate for Mia's young spirit. Jane stood by her side, holding Sarah's elbow to guide her through the process, Later, Sarah could not recollect who attended. Sarah's musical choice was Adagio for Strings. She heard it once in Schindler's List and knew some consider it the saddest music ever written. As the cello strings soared to their tormented pitch, it matched her tortured soul. Sarah stood by Mia's urn, looking at her prepared piece. She crumpled it, letting it drop.

"A nice woman asked me yesterday if I planned to have a Celebration of Life for Mia. Such dissembling words to sugarcoat her death. I celebrated her life every minute of every day that I shared with my precious child. Mia is gone. If you didn't know she was precious, beautiful, smart, and funny well - it is too late."

"No matter how grief-stricken you are now, tomorrow you will wake up, and your daily grind will start again. Mia celebrated every day too. She loved her school, her friends, her toys, and me. Mia loved me. Tomorrow Mia no longer gets to do those things.,

Sarah wavered, and Jane grabbed her arm and led her out the door.

Jane brought her into her own home and tucked her into bed. Her friend lay next to a sobbing Sarah.

Sarah left before Jane woke up the next morning.

Which Way Do I Go?

The gun weighed heavy in her hand. Quick, easy, and the chemicals and energy of her body would re-enter the earth following Mia's. Sarah loaded the chambers of the gun. She lifted it effortlessly. Before it reached its target, Sarah caught a flash out of the corner of her eye. She lowered the gun and looked towards the brightness. Squinting at the apparition moving towards her appeared to be someone standing in a boat.

Sarah released the gun and stood, shading her eyes to get a better view. A tall woman stood erect in a canoe, paddled by children of all ages.

Am I dead? I don't remember pulling the trigger. The gun lay on the ground, its barrel cool.

The canoe reached the shore and Sarah stared at a native American woman who held herself with regal elegance. Her dress was tanned to a buttery texture. Across the yoke and sleeves were thousands of tiny blue and white beds. Other beads detailed symbolic designs. Her dress ended at mid-knee. Even more extensive beadwork embellished the knee-length moccasins. A simple beaded headband with a feather in the back crowned her head.

One feature transcended the majesty of her dress. Kind black eyes. Eyes that bathed Sarah with rosy light. What makes eyes that kind? They singled her out, making Sarah feel like the most important person in the world.

They bestowed unconditional love on Sarah, right at this moment, no matter what happened. Her eyes radiated total acceptance. "Sarah," she stated in a melodic voice."

"Ho-how do you know my name?" Stammered Sarah.

"We all know each other. I am Buffalo Daughter. You are Sarah the Mother Healer. You bore Beloved Mia. Sarah certainly did not remember a woman such as this but felt inexplicably drawn towards her. The children splashed out of the canoe pulling it to the shoreline. They played in the cold water. Their laughter rose affixed to the droplets which fell shimmering into the lake. Sarah thought that their presence would be upsetting. Instead, the children lit the lake with joy.

"Am I dead?"

"Not dead as you thought you would be," White Buffalo nodded towards the gun. "You are still on this earth, just not of this earth.

"I don't understand..." Sarah looked into the woman's eyes, meeting the kindness. What is it about kindness that touches your heart more than any other emotion? Tears welled in her eyes.

"Why are you here?" asked Sarah.

"I ask you to travel. Your grief causes an imbalance in our Spirit World. There may be another path for you, though you must decide if it is yours." Sarah looked at the trail behind her. Only pain and grief lay there. She looked down at the gun. Instant relief lay in the bullets. She hesitated.
Buffalo Daughter felt her indecision. "Let me give you a little help." She lifted, Sarah's hand to her cool cheek. Kindness shattered the grief around her again The intolerable pain lifted, enough that Sarah could see, feel, and hear again.

Her indecision waned. "I will try." Sarah stepped into the canoe, catching her foot and causing the boat to rock precariously. The children clamored into the canoe padding them to the little stand of trees that separated the two lakes.

"There is an archway here that may offer a path that will balance the Spirit World. It remains open as long as your desire is clear. I gave you my grace when you touched my cheek. It will not last, you must find your peace.

"Will you be there to help me?"

"The Spirit connects us all; it will come in many different forms."

This may be good, or it may be very bad.

"Walk next to that little crooked tree. Follow the path down the mountain. A new journey will begin."

Sarah pushed through the twisted subalpine fir. There was a shimmer like you get with a migraine. Once through she found herself on the original side of the lake. Confused, Sarah headed down the familiar trail. Except the trail seemed a little off. It narrowed and lost its edges. Sarah had to backtrack a few times to find it. The trees appeared different somehow. The rock formations remained the same, but the trail disappeared at times. The little creeks curved differently through the fields.

Sarah only made it down because she knew the original path so well. The bottom posed another problem. When Sarah's hiking boots should have hit her in a paved parking lot, the dirt trail continued. She thought she was confident of the way but now felt confused. A small rough-shod abandoned cabin added to her befuddlement. The road turned muddy. Here and there stood more cabins. Some stood close to the road; others trucked back in the hills. A few cabins were dimly lit. Would she be safe in the strange place?

Around twilight, Sarah arrived at a small town. Not a modern burg, but a place only seen in pictures of the old west. Rutted tracks scarred the muddy streets. The smell of horse manure wafted to her wrinkled nose. The buildings sometimes looked like cabins. Other sported tall exteriors hiding little rooms in the back. Many buildings offered wooden porches to help people avoid the mud. Where was she? When was she? Where had White Buffalo sent her? Most importantly, what was she supposed to do now? Thirst, hunger, and fatigue overwhelmed her. One building appeared lively with laughter and lights. With shaky legs, Sarah headed towards her only choice.

Stay or Go?

A woman met Sarah at the door dressed in clothes matching the town's old west theme. A corset sculpted her hourglass figure. A long red silk dress flaunted flounces and lace. The perilous neckline threatened to spill her girls. "What have we here?" the women surveyed Sarah. "You look like a girl, but you sure don't dress like one. If you are trying to pass like a boy, you are doing one poor job."

Sarah felt ill, needing help. She started the first of her many lies to come. "I think I fell and hit my head. I can't remember anything."

"What's your name," demanded the woman.

Sarah looked blank. Easy to do feeling so sick. "I - I don't remember."

The woman pulled Sarah into the well-lit house peering at her, "You do look pretty poorly Why are you wearing pants?"
"I don't know." The room began to spin.

"Who are your folks?" Before Sarah could form another lie, she crumpled onto the floor. She awoke on a sofa. The occupants of the house might call it a settee. A young woman with soft white skin marred by harsh makeup tried to help her drink. Sarah took a gulp, then spluttered.

Whiskey? Why would they give her whisky?

"Can I have a glass of water, please?"

"Sure, I thought the whiskey would perk you up faster, you know?" Sarah didn't know but nodded her head anyway. The girl brought the water which Sarah drained from the cold clear glass. Her stomach gurgled.

The woman from the front door appraised her again. "Do you remember your name now?"

"It's Sarah, Sarah."

"My name is Miss Ellie. This is my boarding house and my girls. I don't like to see any girl in trouble. Maybe your people will find you if you stay here a few days."

"I-I'd appreciate it very much." Sarah began looking around. Her settee sat in a small room. In concurrence with the word settee, she would call this room a parlor. She heard piano music and laughter jangling from a room next door.

"Are you hungry? Are you well enough to eat?"

"I think I became sick because I haven't eaten in a while."

"I thought you didn't remember anything." Miss Ellie was sharp. Sarah needed to be on her toes. The young girl brought Sarah a large bowl of some type of stew and a mug of beer. "I hate to be trouble, but could I please have another glass of water?" Sarah dug into the stew. The rich fair featured venison. Sarah disliked the gamey taste but didn't complain as she finished the bowl. Miss Ellie sat next to her. "I suspect you will have a bit of story to tell me. But I see your eyelids are drooping. I'll let you stay in one of the rooms tonight; then we can sort things out in the morning."

"Thank you for your kindness. I'm not sure what I would have done. I will feel better in the morning and can get out of your way." Miss Ellie led Sarah up a set of stairs.

Young women were laughing and drinking with the men. Some danced to raucous tunes. She remembered Miss Ellie saying boarding house and my girls. Oh my God, I am in a whore house? Her stomach clenched so hard she feared losing her supper.

Ellie opened the door to Sarah's room. It had a simple iron bedstead. The covers looked gray and dirty. Sarah's real nightmare began when she pulled them back. The filthy bottom sheet made Sarah gag. Disgusting wetness stained the middle of the sheet. Sarah did not have to add two plus that the moist stain was the product of the prostitute's work. What would the mattress look like? I cannot sleep here. Pulling the top covers back, they held the telltale stain, though dry. *Ohmygod, ohmygod, ohmygod*, what am I going to do? Sleep on the floor? Mouse droppings in the corner nixed that idea.

Despair set in as the door opened. The pale girl handed her linens. "Miss Ellie thought you might want these." Sarah sighed in relief. Doubling the sheets and blankets, her body lay as far from the mattress as possible. Easing into the lumpy bed, Sarah slept in the crook of her arm. Oh, please no bed bugs.

John watched his friend and ranch hand amble down the road back to his own cabin. John and Bill often sat on the porch discussing the day's work news from the town interspersed with a few old memories. Sometimes they said nothing, taking in the pink/purple sunset behind the great mountain. Loathing to go into the lonely cabin, John sat outside until dark. Finally, he lit the kerosene lantern, opening the door. The light brightened the table, but cast shadows on the rest of the interior. John picked up a small gray daguerreotype looking at the two faces. One dearly familiar, one only known inside his heart. His Father and Mother. Of course, he knew the man that raised him. Faither was strict when teaching John how to work, not sparing a sharp tongue or a leather strap when needed. On the reverse, he showed John how to play, how to fish, how to hunt, and how to sit quiet to enjoy their blessings. They were Quakers, part of a Scottish congregation that migrated to the west. But with no other Quakers in town, his father taught him the ways of the church on their homestead. The most important thing faither taught John was how to be a good man.

Mother, well that was different. As a young boy, Faither told him that his Mother died when he was very young. John accepted the story. He didn't miss what he never knew. Faither hired Mrs. Flanagan to cook and clean Though she thought well of the boy, she didn't believe her job included mothering.
John grew up, attending school. Faither adamantly insisted that his boy receive an education. Often Faither looked drawn and exhausted in the evening.

"I'll do the horses tonight," said John.

"Do ye have schoolwork?"

"Yes sir."

"Then ye best be getting to it," Faither would say, walking out of the cabin back to the chores. Faither withheld a secret from John. He wanted to tell the boy, but John never seemed the right age. He was too young at five, he wasn't mature enough at ten. Faither wondered if John. would ever be old enough. Secrets have a way of working themselves into daylight and this one did, too.

Sixth-year school found John at recess, Big for his age, nobody teased him. Except for Bill. Bill Redd never lost a chance to taunt John. It was nothing serious. "You're so ugly you need a new hat to cover your face. You're so ugly you are a hayseed," said Bill, forcing John to look down to pick the straw off his clothes. John flushed and moved threateningly toward his irritating schoolmate. John had a good four inches on Bill at the time. But Bill didn't run away, rather crowding in, preventing a good punch .He taunting continued, not daily, but at least weekly. One day Bill said, "You're so ugly your morn died giving birth to you." John didn't just flush, he turned bright red. He pushed Bill away, landing a fist to Bill's right eye. Bill didn't back down swinging his fist into John's nose. "Fight! Fight!" yelled the children as they circled the two boys scuffling.

The headmaster ran out, grabbing the boys by their collars separating them. "What's this about?"

"He hit me first," said Bill through a quickly swelling eye.

Stay or Go?

"That's cuz he said my mom died birthing me," said John spitting out blood. The headmaster stood quiet, and so did some of the children. John looked, seeing their faces.

"Geez John, I thought you knew. I was saying it to be mean, I didn't know you....," Bill trailed off. John broke loose from the headmaster's grip, ran to his horse, and raced back to the homestead. He found his father in the barn.

"Is it true? Is it true? Did Mother die because of me?"

"Why are you bleeding everywhere, did ye get into a fight? The belt will be ready if you were fighting at school."

"Faither!" John yelled. Then quiet, "Is it true I killed mother when she birthed me?

All the air went out of his father. He handed John a rag to wipe his nose then pulled him over to the hay bales. "Nae, it is not true."

"But Bill said---"

"Your mother died when ye were born. But you dinnae kill her. You had nothing to do with her death. Sometimes women die when they have babies. It is a dangerous thing having babes. That's what happened to Mother."

John's 12-Year-old brain couldn't wrap around this concept. "I killed her, I killed her," he sobbed.

"Hush. Remember when the black cow tried to give birth, but the calf laid wrong? Remember the cow died?

"But the calf died too. I didn't die."

"No, your Mother sacrificed herself for the precious gift of you. I think about her every day. You know I fell in love with your mother the instant I met her. I knew I was going to marry her. I wish I had Mother and yours both, but God gave me the precious gift of a son."

Back at school Bill came up to John, kicking dirt in front of his feet "John, I'm really sorry about what I said; it was mean whether you knew about it or didn't."

"Go away Bill, it's over." But it wasn't Just as Bill pulled in close for a fight, he pulled in even closer to be a friend. John couldn't shake him, and one day realized that the two were inseparable. It took many years for John to understand the death of his Mother and work out his guilt. Peace was hard won.

Sarah awoke with the light of day. Mia's absence burst through her first thoughts. The pain that Buffalo Daughter lifted started to disappear. This solution seemed worse than the prospect of the gun. She clutched the spirit of Mia tightly in her heart. Sarah headed out of the bedroom, knowing there was a lot of storytelling to do. She followed her nose to the dining room. Miss Ellie and six young girls, in various stages of dress, sat around the table, chatted, and ate.

"Well there she is!" exclaimed Miss Ellie. Most girls appraised her and then fell back to gossiping. Introductions rounded the table. Sarah, in her jeans and wrinkled shirt, held little interest in their small world. Two sets of eyes kept their gaze though. Adele the pale girl who helped Sarah last night stared. Another young woman Kat bore her eyes into Sarah, making her uncomfortable. "I didn't think you'd ever wake. You slept 18 hours straight," said Miss Ellie.

Sarah shook her head in disbelief. "What is the date?"

"Why honey it is Friday the 21st."

But what year?

Sarah never breakfasted in a brothel before. O.K., she had never been in a brothel before. She eyed the occupants at the table. Miss Ellie dressed in a severe black dress, with ruffles in the front that ran from her double chin to under her considerable breasts. When Miss Ellie stood, Sarah saw the dress sported a complicated bustle of ruffles. Her body was stuffed tight into the dress. So tight that Sarah doubted her arms could raise to her shoulders. Her hair was pulled severely to the top of her head, then set into curls. She looks like a frilly black sausage. The girls, on the other hand, were colorful jewels on a crown. Chinese red, flamingo pink, emerald green, and brilliant blue colored their robes and gowns. Some wore loosely laced corsets under an oriental-style robe. Others chose satin dresses, loose and draped low off their shoulders. Exotic shawls covered their necks from the chill. It seemed all had a distinct style. I guess a different flavor for every man. Their hair colors varied. Some seemed natural; a few were bleached. Some had artificial single-toned black. One girl brushed her hair into two high ponytails. Her short dress was designed as for a child. Sarah sickened at the thought of what men wanted this girl.

Cigarette smoke filled the room. Sarah's throat felt hot. The women were as now as curious about Sarah as she was about them. Breakfast was served; temporary chaos reigned as everybody demanded their share. It looked to Sarah like there was plenty to go around. A cacophony of voices filled the room as they ate. Table manners were in short supply.

"Sally, I saw you had two goes at old Ned last night."

"Yeah, he was right frisky. Bastard only tipped me once though."

"I thought there was going to be a fight over who got Nelly first!"

"George hates seconds. Good thing Miss Ellie distracted that other guy with some beer."

Seconds?

"Aren't you eating anything Gillie?"

"No, I'm on the whiskey diet. I've lost three days already." The dry humor set the group laughing.

Sarah's stomach demanded to eat the hearty fare in front of her. Crisp bacon, greasy-looking eggs, ham, and biscuits. Everything tasted good, but when Sarah bit into the buttered biscuit, she thought her mouth had gone to heaven. She reached for another. She debated a third, but Kat piped, "I guess some don't worry about girlish figures." Kat eyed Sarah's clothes and the other girls tittered.

"Well now, enough of that," said Miss Ellie, all business-like now. "Tell us Sarah, where do your folks hail from?"

Thank goodness Mike watched those detective shows. Sarah remembered a few important principles of lying. Base your lie on as much truth as possible. Do not offer more than what the question asks. Don't embellish with extraneous information. That will trip you up every time. "Scranton, Kansas." Good start. Her parents had lived in Kansas. Nobody would know all the towns in Kansas in 2022 much less now.

"I don't believe I have ever heard of Scranton."

"It's a small town in eastern Kansas."

"What brings you out here?"

"Father was a missionary, and he wanted to bring the word of God to the west."

"He couldn't preach in Scranton?"

"I guess he thought he had converted everybody he could there." The girls laughed.

"How about your Momma?"

"Mother? She taught school then married Father." That lie was good. Many women taught school before marriage.

"Where are they now?"

Sarah thought of Mia, her only family, and real tears started. "We were going to stay with Aunt Florence, but my parents died with the fever on the way. I tried to find her, but they told me they moved to San Francisco for some mining adventure."

"How did you get here?"

Sarah had no idea where here was. "I - I don't know. I came down with the fever, and don't remember."

"You said you hit your head on a rock."

"Did I?" Remember, not too much information.

"You speak well, you must have had schooling."

"Mother taught me." Sarah veered from the rules of lying and purposefully supplemented this answer. It may be a way to survive. "My Father was a doctor, too."

"A missionary and a doctor at the same time, that is unusual," said Miss Ellie, pouncing on the lie.

"He started as a doctor until the word of the Lord struck him. But missionary work pays poorly, so he kept practicing medicine to support us." Now Sarah embellished the lie to plant the seed. "With Mother's teaching complete, he began educating me about medicine. I'm not a full physician, just an apprentice physician." Sarah remembered in the west that doctors were scarce and often studied under another medical practitioner.

72

"So, we should call you Dr. Sarah?"

"That would be pretentious at this stage. There are a lot of gaps in my training." Despite her protestations, the name Dr. Sarah stuck.

Miss Ellie clapped her hands. "It's time girls. It's Saturday night, and we have work to do!" Some jumped up and some drug their chairs. Sarah figured Saturday night would be the busiest night of the week at a brothel. Miss Ellie and Adele approached Sarah.

"You can't go around in those filthy trousers. Adele, get one of those old dresses and show Sarah where to wash. She'll need help with her buttons."

Adele chattered cheerfully as Sarah peeled off her dirty clothes. "I ain't never met to lady doctor before." Sarah wanted to protest the moniker but concerned herself about privacy during her bath.

"Uh, do we have that dress?'

"Oh sure, I done forgot that."

Sarah washed as fast as she could, barely finishing before Adele returned. The dress shrugged over Sarah's head. Adele began buttoning, but it gaped at the waist. Despite tugging hard, the buttons would not meet in the middle. "Don't you have a corset?" Sarah never owned Spanx, much less a corset. Adele created a solution by buttoning the dress above and below the waist, giving Sarah a shawl to wrap around the gap.

Which Way Do I Go?

John's father sent him to a high school in town. His keen mind needed more tutelage than the local school provided. The new headmaster introduced him to the law, beginning his studies and interest in legal work. It took a number of years, but the lawyer used his influence to gain John's admission to his alma mater. His father sold off a section of his precious land. John found himself on a train to Greensboro Law School.

The world tilted a bit for John when he disembarked. He was used to wagons and carriages, just not that many going so fast. Everybody walked or rode in a hurry. He expected the large number of buildings. He anticipated the numbers of people. It was hard to absorb so much activity in such a close space.

John made his way to a livery. His practiced eye picked out a horse with good formation and spirit. Asking directions, he road to the school. His classmates seemed like upright young men. Their deep southern drawl forced him to concentrate, hoping he could understand half of what was said. How would he understand the lectures?

The gentlemen were initially interested in him. Unfortunately, he stood out sharply. On the advice of the local shopkeeper in Montana, he ordered "city" clothes. He didn't know what city she thought he was going to reside, but it surely was not North Carolina. He would have to telegraph Faither for funds for clothes that didn't stand out.

"That's some hat you have there." The other young men snickered. "Where are you from?"

"Montana Territory." That got their attention. They peppered him with questions. Once they found out that the Indian Wars were over, and General Custer was indeed dead, they lost interest. John found himself standing to the side of the group.

A well-dressed young woman with an intelligent face moved towards him.

"How are the Indians faring with the reservation system? Do you think the Dawes Act will pass?"

John looked with surprise at the lady. She wasn't a classic beauty, but her pleasant face and sparkling eyes signaled intelligence.

"I didn't think anybody who lived east of the Mississippi knew anything about the Dawes Act. said John. Do you work here?"

"I'm Elena. I am your classmate," she smiled.

"Can't say I'm surprised, but something tells me you can run circles around us men." John, who was a little out of place back east, and Elena, totally out of place as a women in man's territory, began a friendship. School started. The male classmates warmed up to John, enjoying his friendly persona. Some were especially grateful as he always extended a helping hand with a difficult chapter. The relationship with Elena warmed up too. They spent many study nights together when the topic drifted off law and into other pleasant thoughts.

The men's favorite topic of conversation was the war. "If only General Jackson had done this" and "If only that damn General Sherman hadn't raped their land," accompanied by a spit to the ground. "Can you stand these darkies walking around like they owned the place?"

John steered clear of the talk. The political tensions of the day made it impossible. "What unit did your father serve, John?"
He hesitated. "Faither had a deferment." He waited for the blow back, but none came. All the well-off student's fathers bought a deferment from the war.

The inevitable occurred late in the first quarter. The students drank heavily one night, looking for trouble. John came upon them beating a terrified black man. He instinctively ran into the group, throwing them off their victim, taking and giving punches as good as he got. Finally, they stopped. John kept his fists up, breathing heavily, sweat, and blood dripping down his face.

"Are you a nigger lover?" asked his classmate, hate dripping from his mouth.

I am a Quaker, and yes, I am an abolitionist." John dropped to his knees, nausea and dizziness overcoming him. His classmates left him on the street. Clearly intelligence, knowledge, and passion meant nothing in a career of law. Just your standing on a war from almost 20 years ago. The young men shunned John. Elena's family forbid her from talking to him. One morning the Dean summoned John to his office. His law career teetered on the edge of disaster. But true catastrophe came in the form of a telegram. Faither was dead.

Sarah walked down the stairs, catching Miss Ellie's eye. Cleaned up, Sarah's natural prettiness shone through, Clear skin, pink lips on a mouth a little wide for her face with a smattering of freckles made her an attractive woman. The long chestnut hair tied back with a ribbon launched her from attractive to beautiful. Miss Ellie knew more than one man would pay well for a woman like that. "Educated, too," she mused. "I might make some money on this chit."

"Come over here dear, sit with me."

"I thought I would take leave now; I have put you through enough trouble."

"No, no trouble at all. Let me get this all written out." Miss Ellie scratched on a piece of paper.

Sarah looked around on the desk and found her jackpot-a calendar. According to Mack's Mercantile, it was May 21, 1882, in Beautiful Horse Country Jordan, Montana Territory. Jordan was the small town that burned in the early 1900's. What happened in 1882? She frantically searched her mind. The Civil War had ended. When were the Indian Wars over? The President was... Maybe knowing how people lived with their technology would be more useful. The apprentice physician lie may help her earn a wage. What was medicine like now?

Miss Ellie handed her a small piece of paper with figures written in a scrawl. Sarah squinted her eyes, but could not make it out

"What does this say?"

"I thought you could read, dearie."

"I am having a hard time with your handwriting."

Miss Ellie, offended, said, "That is your bill."

"My - my bill."

"Of course. This is a boarding house, not a charity home. Let me make sure I charged you correctly. Two nights stay, $2 per night. Two meals, 50 cents each. One dress. It is old, so I only charged you $2. Oh- clean linen service, 25 cents. The total is $8.25.

"I have no money."

"I thought with your father being a physician you would be holding onto some cash."

"No, I do not have one red cent! I am an apprentice physician. I can find some cases then pay you. I promise I will pay you in full."

"I am supposed to trust a girl I have never seen with a poorly made up story return with a payment? I don't think so Missy."

"I can clean the boarding house for you for a week?"

"I have a cleaning woman."
"I can help in the kitchen."

"Cora cooks and needs no help."

Sarah wracked her brain. Sewing! "I know how to sew. I can repair dresses and linens."

"That is a tempting offer, but Mrs. Jones does that for me. She is widowed with three children. You wouldn't want to take work from her, would you?"

"You cannot keep me here. I will find a way to repay you."

"Where are you going, girl? Miss Ellie asked sharply, blocking Sarah's path.

"You can't leave here until you pay the bill."

"You can't keep me here a prisoner. It's against the law."

"Let's call my dear friend Office Ryan. He gets paid with a friendly girl in return for our protection. I am sure he can settle this matter. If he comes here, you will end up in jail for prostitution and thieving until you can pay. Maybe you could be his friendly girl tonight."

Sarah finally realized where this was going. "How may I ask, do you propose I pay this bill?"

"Why it is easy. All you must do is entertain the gentlemen. Two or three weekends and your bill will be paid." Why had Sarah put her faith into an Indian apparition? A ghost Indian Shaman invoked even less trust than any other God. Fooled again. She landed in the dangerous world of prostitution. She believed Mia's dying represented the most she could bear. Yet here she stood alive. A whore with no legal rights in 1882. Sarah set her sights on survival.

Adele patted her hand. "It h'aint so bad, Dr. Sarah. The first one is the hardest. But it gets easier. You are so pretty that Miss Ellie will charge high dollar for you. You only have to be with the rich men."
"How do you do this Adele? How does it work?"

"H'aint you ever been with a man Dr. Sarah?"

"Yes, yes, I don't mean that. But how does it work here?"

"You go out to the bar and pick a man you want to be with. Mostly they pick you though. You take them to your room; then they have you. You go back downstairs and do it all over."
"How do you protect yourself? Like from getting sick? Or pregnant?"

"We have them rubbers, but most men won't wear them. I ask them to, but they just laugh."

"How many men a night?"

"Oh, on a good night 6 or 7."

Dear God.

"How much do you make each time?"

"About three dollars. Miss Ellie takes half. We gets to keep the tips. She sez it makes us work harder so the men come back lookin' for more. This h'aint a high class city parlor, but we be safe and clean. Miss Ellie don't charge us much for room and board, Adele frowned. But the bills keep adding up, it's hard to make enough money to leave.

Adele's story told Sarah everything she needed to know. Miss Ellie trapped girls into prostitution then kept them too impoverished to leave. Some had to go somehow. There were only six girls. Sarah wondered what it would take to leave this place.

I need an escape plan.

John did not remember the trip home, keeping his grief stuffed inside his gullet. It only rose to the surface when he rode through the iron archway to the homestead. Faither built it when John was a boy. McIntyre & Son. The grief held in for 2000 miles cascaded from his soul. Never was he more alone than now.
Bill waited for him by the cabin. John wiped the heartache from his face. "I'm so sorry, John. Your dad was like a father to me. I know that doesn't compare to what you feel, but I do understand some." John led the horse to the barn. They sat on the haystacks.

"I never got to say goodbye. I didn't get to tell Faither I loved him. I have nothing left of him.

"You have a huge part of your father here. You have the homestead. The land he worked every day of his life. This homestead he cherished and intended to hand down to you. This place needs you." John clung to the sage advice like a drowning man.

John immediately jumped into the work on the homestead, vowing to make his father proud. The work was a balm on his heart and helped him live without his father.

One night he lifted the old picture of his father and mother. John put down the daguerreotype. He scooted the Shaker chair he was making over by the fire, beginning to sand the curved edge of the back. Work wouldn't banish his loneliness tonight. He stirred the stew on the stove but found it scorched from the high heat. That didn't matter, he wasn't hungry either. The ghosts in the empty room began closing in. John grabbed his hat. He couldn't stay here tonight. Saddling his horse, he headed into town.

Arriving at the saloon he tied his mount. He could hear the laughter of the girls at Miss Ellie's. No, he wasn't going to take that route tonight. In the saloon, most of the seats were filled with the Saturday night regulars. "Hey John, come sit over here with us." John shook his head. Right now, he wanted to be a spectator rather than a participant to the cacophony in the bar. He had a strange feeling of being in the room, it not part of the room.

He swung a leg over a barstool. "Whiskey." The first sip proved the owner still stocked their rot gut special. John knew the second shot would be better. He observed a card game and saw every man cheat, then accuse each other of being lying crooks of the lowest kind. John heard the tinkle of women's laughter again. He shoved down his longing, asking for another whiskey. The second shot tasted as bad as the first. He stood up and jammed his hat on his head. Why shouldn't he enjoy the gentle voices and soft skin of the women? Besides, Miss Ellie's whiskey was better.

A girl looked through the window and let out a high squeal. "It's John!" The prostitutes rushed to the window verifying the exciting event. Sarah nudged her way through the group in time to see a man approach the brothel. There must be a half a dozen of John's in town, but clearly, this John stood out.

"Who is John?" she whispered to Adele who appeared to be all aflutter.

"He is a special customer. He only comes in two or three times a year. He doesn't chew." Sarah had not considered that habit when she thought of entertaining the men. "He is really nice to us girls. He makes us feel like we is special. He tips good, too."

Adele's face dropped when Kat came over, face in high color. "I'll wear my pink dress tonight. John likes me in pink, he done told me that last time."

Adele said to Sarah with a twisted face. "I don't know why I get my hopes up. He usually chooses Kat cuz she is the prettiest. He h'aint never chosen me. Maybe this time...."

Miss Ellie swooped into the room, her business mind calculating. "It looks like we will entertain a special visitor tonight." The girls murmured excitedly. "Kat, of course, he usually chooses you." Kat preened like a proud peacock. "We have a new exotic bird with us tonight, too. Someone fresher."

A bird locked in a gilded cage.

"Kat, give Sarah your gold dress. It will look good with her eyes. And give her a new corset, too."

The girls scurried to their rooms. Kat threw the gold dress and an old corset at Sarah. Sarah looked at each piece of clothing, bewildered. God bless Adele who came in to rescue her. Adele wrapped the corset around Sarah's waist. She fastened the hooks above and below the waist.

Now is the time for the rubber to hit the road.

Sarah grimaced. With insistent hands, Adele worked the cording tighter and ever tighter. "You have to stop; I can't get my breath."

Adele nodded dubiously. "We have a ways to go Dr. Sarah."
In the end, the corset pulled tight enough that the gold silk dress fit, though strained, at the waist. Sarah knew there would be no eating or drinking. She unsuccessfully tried a deep breath. No wonder women fainted.

"Hurry! He's here!"

Sarah tried to descend the staircase with dignity. That had to be the famous John sitting with the gaggle of girls. John sat in a chair. Kat perched on the bench closest to him, refilling his glass of whiskey. Her pink gown dove to her navel. Maybe an exaggeration, but she was sure John had a clear view of Kat's own girls.

Clumsily, Sarah's foot caught in the hem of the dress. She managed to grab the banister for her balance in a very unladylike manner. John noticed her stumble with a friendly grin. Winning might mean an early ticket out of here. Losing meant these disgusting tobacco-chewing men would get a go at her. Competing against Kat's soft charms seemed futile. What did she have that Kat did not? A fresh face afforded an advantage. Watching Kat, it dawned on her that maybe intelligence and humor might be the answer.

Sarah made her way down the stairs through the group. John may not have been a romance book Scottish warrior, but he would do very nicely. His pleasant face sported a relaxed smile. His lower lip was full, the upper hidden by a-well-groomed mustache and beard. Sarah loved his light brown hair, wavy and combed back from his face. When John looked at her, she noticed his eyes. Their hazel matched perfectly. Two sets of brown and green with flecks of gold. "How unusual," she said. "We have the same color of eyes."

"I've never noticed the color of my eyes."

A girl ran to find a mirror. John gazed at his eyes for a second, then looked at Sarah's. "You are right." He checked again. "How unusual for hazel eyes to match.

Sarah took in a deep breath. OK a deep a breath as the damn corset would allow. "I'm Sarah."

"You must be new here I'm Sarah."

"Oh, I would say I am pretty new."

New to your century.

"Yes, yes I came in last night."

From 2022

She tried the widest smile she could, but knew it looked fake. Stick to the plan, stick to the plan.

Kat brushed a soft breast across his muscled upper arm. Her hand already lay intimately on his thigh. Time to step up the game.

"Do I detect a bit of a Scottish brogue?"

"I dinnae think my talk was oobvious, no?"

"Ach no, I hear a wee bit. No other couldnae hear."

John laughed in return. "My grandfather was Scottish. He immigrated here in 1802."

"Has he passed?

"Aye." My Faither's accent changed slowly, but my education taught me the perfect English accent.

"But you nae forgit," she teased.

"Nae," he chuckled.

Kat looked less sure of herself. She tugged on John's hand, whispering in his ear, "Johnny, how about going upstairs now?"

Sarah moved quickly. "Tell me about your grandfather."

John gave her his full attention. "What a firebrand! He sharecropped a farm in Scotland. When the drought came, the crops failed. The Lairds demanded the same share of crops. Whole villages starved. Scotland held no future for him, so he sailed for America. He landed in a large Scottish settlement in Wisconsin. Grandda was no afraid of hard work. It took five years, but he pinched every penny…"

"-as Scotsmen are known to do." Sarah interrupted with a twinkle.

"Aye as us Scotsmen are known to do. He traveled here buying the most beautiful and lush section of land in the valley," he said with pride.

"I bet he missed Scotland."

"He missed the people, the lochs and even the harsh weather."

"I've been to Scotland," she ventured.

"You have?" His hazel eyes drilled into her with fascination.

Kat said, "You are makin' it up."

"No really, when I was much younger, my grandparents were well to do. We flew, -uh sailed to Scotland for a long summer vacation, uh, I mean holiday." Except for the sailing part, this was true. Sarah joined a high school trip touring Scotland.

"I have always wanted to return to my ancestral land. Where did you go?"

Since everything in Scotland was centuries old, Sarah figured she could expand freely on this topic. Sarah mused a space next to John, effectively blocking Kat's access. "Of course, Edinburgh Castle is where everybody wanted to go. The castle impressed everybody, including me. Every tourist had to see the Loch Ness monster." She cited:

A visitor once to Loch Ness
Met the monster, which left him a mess.
They returned his entrails
By their regular mails
And the rest by pony express.

The entire room erupted in laughter, but none louder than John.

"I have to keep my eye on you."

"Seriously though, I loved the faraway places," said Sarah, suddenly taken back to the time of the vacation. "It is Eilean Donan that captured my spirit. I still have a picture of the castle in my head. I think the story that captivated me the most is when the son of the original clan acquired the power to talk to birds. That would be a fantastic power. I would love to talk to birds."

"My grandfather often spoke of Eilean Donan." John and Sarah put their heads together talking about the ruined castle.

Miss Ellie disapproved of the serious talk. "Why are we talking about the olden days?"

John smiled, "You are right, too much talk of Scotland. You know, I was once mocked for being insufficiently Scottish. They actually threatened to have me kilt." Sarah started to laugh at the pun, but it came out as an un-lady like snort.
"I told them, "Anyone who forces me to wear a kilt should be tartan feathered."

Laughter, suppressed for so long, bubbled out of Sarah. "You are bad," taking a pretend swat at his head.

"I dinnae know what you mean."

"Much better!' exclaimed Miss Ellie. "I think it is time to choose."
John stood to survey the women. First, he scowled at Sarah. "You laugh too much."
I am a good actress.

He winked at blushing Kat. He wandered to Adele with a kind smile, chucking her under her chin. She thrilled at the attention. He wandered back to the beginning. Hazel eyes met hazel eyes as his mouth descended on hers. His lips were moist and soft. The taste of warm whiskey lingered on his tongue. His beard brushed her cheek. A small erotic sound emitted from the back of her throat. Without thinking, her arms rose to his neck."

"We have a winner!" The men in the room clapped and stomped their boots.

John moved to a corner with Miss Ellie. Sarah, still under the influence of the kiss, saw John open his wallet handing Miss Ellie money. smiled a protest, so he doubled his payment.

Kat hissed at Sarah, "John is mine. You will pay for this."

John grasped Sarah's hand leading her up the staircase. He knew the way, opening the door to an airy, well-furnished clean room. "I need another appetizer," he murmured, pulling Sarah closer to him at her waist. Bending over slightly, his soft mouth pressed into hers. Moving his head back and forth caused his mustache to tickle her lips. She drew his wavy hair closer to her lips. John untied the ribbon from her hair. Her long locks slid forward. He picked a curl and tugged. Your hair is not brown or black, what is it?"
"They call it chestnut."
"Hmm. I guess it is."
Sarah's nerves started to freeze. What was she doing? Seducing a man she didn't know? Her only previous partner was Mike. However, she needed to escape and this plan was better than the rest. In for a penny, in for a pound.

Sarah slanted her head to better access his mouth. John seemed surprised at the kiss but did not protest. They stood for a long time, lip against lip, hazel eye meeting hazel eye. Sarah brushed her lips around his mouth. John disengaged, letting his lips linger kiss by kiss down the side of her neck. Stopping at the hollow of her neck and clavicle, he paid due attention to this delicate area. She turned her head, so he could better reach the enervated spot.
Sarah stood to pull his suspenders over his shoulders. He deftly unbuttoned his shirt.

Sarah helped him shrug his shoulders out of his shirt. John had to clear his throat. "I dinna think it is fair that my shirt is gone, but the wee miss is still dressed.

"For the love of God, I do not know why they make women's garments so that you need help to get undressed."

"Och! I be glad to help." He used practiced fingers to undo the tiny buttons.
"You sure managed that easily enough." she observed. John grinned, flashing his white teeth.

The silk slipped down her arms so slowly that every hair on her arm stood at attention. He let go, the dress puddling about her feet. She tried to step delicately away from the golden dress, but of course, entangled her heel and began to trip. John caught her before she fell. "A wee bit clumsy still I see."

Good of him to notice.

She began the not-unpleasant task of disrobing the handsome man. She undressed him more clumsily than he did her dress.

"Not as experienced as me, aye?" Sarah blushed. Sarah went to the low dresser and poured water and soft soap into a basin. Adele warned her this was a way to ward off disease. John stopped her. "I assure you I am clean and disease free. Besides, I don't intend to waste our time on the first half hour, I paid for the whole night.

"The whole night?"

"Yes, the whole entire long night."

This job may not be as bad as she thought, only one man for one night.

Sarah reached behind herself, trying to free herself from the tortuous corset. John lent a practiced hand. "Most girls like to keep their corset on."

"This girl wants this son of a bitch off." She clasped her hands to her mouth, horrified that such a word came out. Ladies did not talk like that in 1882. But she was not exactly a lady tonight. John laughed as he pulled the strings of the corset. The corset loosened until it finally fell forward. Sarah collapsed on the bed with a sigh of relief.

"I take it you don't wear corsets often."

"Um, no, Father thought they were bad for a woman's health."

"I can't for the life of me understand why a woman would change the beautiful shape the God gave her. John's calloused hand soothed the angry red marks. First under her arms, then he skimmed the marks from the boning. He leaned forward and kissed, her, and they both surrendered to the kiss and their pleasure.

Afterwards, it was clear the twin bed did not allow for the comfort of two people. That did not cause pause as Sarah and John remained wrapped in each other's bodies. she looked at John. What had happened? What was this electric, magnetic connection to this man? The same question dwelled in his eyes. Was this the feelings his faither told him about?

"I don't think you have done this before."

"No. I guess you can call me an amateur."

"Amateur prostitute, but not amateur woman. Why are you here?"

"Do you mean what is a nice gal like me doing in a place like this?" John looked blank at the modern film quote. Sarah continued, "Sometimes life drops heavy burdens on your shoulders. It seems we must learn what to do with them. I'm sure you have had similar challenges."

My Faither was killed a year ago."

"I am so sorry, said Sarah, understanding his sorrow.

"I lived in North Carolina when I received the telegram. A drunk Indian killed him.

Sarah pictured painted war horses with bows and arrows. "A battle?"

John half laughed. "No, those times are long gone." He continued bitterly. "Just another liquored up drunk who killed my Faither for no other reason than alcohol."

"Did he fight in the War?"

"No, he was a Quaker and a conscientious objector. Of course, as the war drug on, the Union pressed everybody into service. If you paid a $300 fee someone could fight the war for you. But for Quakers, paying the price meant the same as supporting the war. Faither did not have cash like that anyway; his wealth came from the land. Luckily, Montana's craziness for gold and silver distracted the state from pursuing errant Quakers. So, the situation never came to a head."

"How about your mother."
"She died in childbirth ...with me." Sarah touched his face. "Why were you in North Carolina?"

"Faither always wanted an education for me. I studied here and discovered that I like the law. A senior barrister tutored me. I worked the farm with my Faither during the day, then studied at night. The time came when I needed more advanced work. I gained entrance to Greensboro Law School. Faither was killed before I finished my first quarter. Of course, I came home. The homestead is a demanding mistress."

"Sounds like you arc pulled in two directions."

"I love the law. I want to finish my studies. I love the homestead too. A ranch does not allow for time or energy for anything else.

"You sure seem like you have enough energy tonight," she teased.

John turned so that they could spoon. "I've been saiven up my money. If I knew you were going to be here, I may have saived up another month or so.

John stroked her side. He leaned over to capture another kiss, but her hair blocked his target. He pulled it back, revealing Mia's tattoo. John lightly traced the ornate M. Sarah shivered. "Most ladies don't have beautiful tattoos on their shoulders." Sarah stayed silent. Images of Mia washed through her mind.

Those gold curls. Her hazel eyes. Then nothing. The emptiness always lurked behind her heart. John wrapped Sarah securely in his arms, and they lay quiet for a while. "You are different." Later, John watched her as she slept, lightly moving his hand up and down her back. He felt his heart repositioning itself in his chest, Just like Faither and Mother, he knew he was instantly in love with Sarah.

Sarah did not know how long she dozed. She opened her eyes to see matching hazel eyes watching her.

"I was thinking you know a lot about me, but I don't know anything about you. Except you are not a prostitute. And that you are different somehow."

Sarah could not lie to John. "I can't tell you my story."

"Are you a bank robber on the run? Are you a cattle rustler?"
"Ha-ha. Nothing like that. It is a story that is unbelievable. I am not sure I believe it myself."

"You have me baffled. Do you want to stay here with Miss Ellie?" asked John.

"No!" she said with desperation. I want to find work taking care of people, I am not a full doctor, but I know enough to practice medicine. But leaving Miss Ellie's might be a little – complicated.

"Dr. Hancock serves the two towns by himself. He lives 5 miles out. He is a good doctor, just pressed thin. I do not know if you would be welcome or not. I do know that if anybody in Jordan finds out that you spent one night in this brothel you will never work as a doctor. Sarah blanched.

"Why did you come to Miss Ellie's? asked Sarah.

"Loneliness."

"I can't believe you do not have a girlfriend."

"In my teens, I went to school, came home then worked the homestead with Faither. To be sure I had my eyes on some little fillies. But I was tired. Pretty much the same story in reverse after school. I worked the homestead all day and studied law all night." I met my first girlfriend in law school. Elena came from a well to do family. She didn't get into law school because of her family. But because of her intelligence. We would talk for hours about law, politics, well anything."

"What happened to her?"

"Faither was killed, and I had to come home." John omitted the confrontation in North Carolina.

"Sarah, I want to see you again soon, but it is so busy on the homestead, and it is foaling season. Let's ——-"Sarah knew a brush off when she heard one. She cut off his next sentence. She knew John for what-less than 12 hours? What did she think? Love at first sight in 1882? He would rescue her on a white horse? Did she forget she was only a whore in a whorehouse.

"Of course, you are busy. I hope I'll be busy when I can pay my way out of this brothel. Sarah would not look at him. The right words may come out of her mouth, but she couldn't hide the disappointment on her face. "What happened is that you came to Miss Ellie's. We had a good time tonight. That's all. It's time to get some sleep. She lay on the bed pretending to fall asleep. Thank goodness, she hadn't trusted him with her secret. She listened to his every movement. He put his trousers on. His suspenders jingled then his boots scuffed. Footsteps tapped to the bedside, and then rustling.

My tip.

John walked out the door, closing it silently.

Sarah waited until he left the building. The sun rose as she went to the pitcher, bathing in the cold water. Reaching for the towel, she saw something glint. There lay 2 ten-dollar bills - and two pieces of gold coin.

What did this mean? Did he simply want to help her get out of the brothel? Maybe two gold rings of promise? She shook that silliness out of her head. What it meant was freedom.

Sarah found the old dress with her modern clothes. Creeping downstairs. She placed $10 on the top of the bill on Miss Ellie's desk. The clumsy nib ink caused a blotchy, near illegible note. Sarah wanted to leave on good terms.

Dear Miss Ellie,
I will be taking my leave this morning. Thank you for all the help you provided. I may not have survived the first night without you. I believe the money will compensate the bill with a little extra, to show my gratitude.
Sincerely,
Sarah May

Sarah walked out of the brothel a free woman. Lost in this world, but free. Turning her ear to the town's activity, she found Mack's General store. Mack was serving male customers needing supplies for their day, while Sarah hung back until most of the customers were gone.

"Excuse me."

Mack turned around. "Howdy! You surprised me. Are ya new in town?

"How did you know?"

"Guess I know everybody in these parts, and I ain't seen you before."

"This is an unexpected stop. I am not sure about the lay the land here."

"Are you staying long?"

"I don't know yet. I am looking for a place to live."

"There is only one decent place, and that is Mrs. Sullivan's boarding house." He walked her outside. "Go down three streets, turn left. It is the big white house on the corner. The rooms are clean, the meals are good, and she keeps quiet renters."

"Thank you. Does this town have a bank?"

"Wells Fargo opened a little branch about six months ago. It's there on First Street."

Sarah knew her gold coins needed protection. A bank could be robbed, but she could be looted easier. Who would have change for a gold coin anyway? Wells Fargo still existed in 2022. That may come in handy.

"I would like to attend to business, then come back here to pick out some supplies.

"I'll be mighty glad to help ya."

Sarah found the bank, the smell of its raw pine mixed with dusty ledgers. "Can I help you, Miss?" A little man stood behind the teller's cage. "Yes. I would like to open an account."

The little man looked at Sarah's old dress. "I'm not sure you need our help."

"I need to open an account. Plus, a line of credit. Sarah reached into her pocket placing the two gold coins on the desk.

"Yes, I do think we can help you." Sarah filled out the deposit slips, still struggling with the pen. He probably thinks I am illiterate. He handed her the paper for the credit. She figured her pieces of gold were worth about $1200 in modern money. That sounded like a lot, but she didn't know. Leaving the bank, she found Mrs. Sullivan sweeping the porch of her boarding house. "Good morning!" said Sarah, pasting on a smile. "Good morning to you, too." "Mack from the general store told me that you run a very nice boarding house."

"So nice of Mack to say that."

"l am looking for a place to live. Do you have a room available?"

Mrs. Sullivan looked at Sarah's worn dress. "I charge $9 a week, two weeks payable up front. That includes breakfast and dinner. I only allow good Christian women.

That last might be a problem.

Sarah repeated her original story about her missionary parents and the fever.

Mrs. Sullivan's doubtful face turned into one of sympathy. "I have the perfect room for you on the second floor. It faces out to the prairies side of town. Come, I will show you.

It would be better than the brothel.

The clean room contained a bed, a straight chair, and two small dressers. A pitcher and basin stood ready for sponge baths. A kerosene lamp sat on a table. Sarah had no idea how to light it. Homey touched decorated the room. A doily accented a chair. A needlework sampler hung on the floral wallpaper. A beautiful quilt covered the bed.

"Did you make this quilt? How beautiful."

Mrs. Sullivan smiled with pleasure. "I make all the quilts. I snip up every spare piece of fabric to make them. I'll cut a square from your dress if you aren't looking. They both laughed.

"If you will have me, I will pay three month's rent. Sarah had no idea how long she would stay, but three months should give her plenty of time to determine her path.

Mrs. Sullivan looked surprised, but was happy to take to offer.

"Do you have any luggage?"

"I lost everything. I'm going to Mack's to stock up."

"You poor girl, we will take good care of you here.

Sarah walked back to Mack's. She sorely missed the convenience of a car. Even the Harley would be good. She pictured Mike on the Harley running cruising the dusty roads.

I'm back Mack."

I'm glad to see ya. What can I get for you?"

"I'd like to walk around first, if you don't mind."

"Take all the time you want." Mack went back to sorting new stock items.

The store overwhelmed Sarah. It contained everything known to God, and a few more things than that. The counters were organized so that similar items were together. Fifty and 100 pound bags of sugar and flour were propped in one area. Canned goods stood in ordered lines atop the shelves. Though Sarah disliked cigarette smoke, the open pouches of tobacco wafted aromatic flavors. Shoes, boots and other clothing occupied another section. Sarah noted the absence of women's dresses. No matter, her current dress could serve as a pattern she could use to sew. Unusable fashion boots lay on the shelf; Sarah needed something sturdier. Working boots were unwieldy black leather. She hoped her modern hiking boots would last. Another counter displayed patent medicines. She would return to explore the contents. A lower shell held an array of candy. The placement had more to do with children's eye level than storage, Sarah mused. A large back section stocked everything a homesteader could ever need. John must stop here regularly.

Now Sarah, she chided herself.

She dictated her order to Mack. A watch, various soaps, tooth powder, tooth and hairbrush, gold and green calico (only 10 cents a yard!), scissors, thread, two simple chemises, a nightgown, and four pairs of knickers. Sarah blushed at that, but Mack went on filling the stock like he heard this every day. Which he probably did. Socks were a problem. They were knee length, thick knitted wool, or light fashion models.

Can they be altered? How many years until they invent synthetic knits?

Hat and gloves rounded out the order. The store did. It stock tampons, maxi-pads or anything else related to a woman's menstrual cycle. God, that sounded like a mess. Maybe Mrs. Sullivan would help.

After the long order, she eyed the candy. How long had it been since she had anything sweet. Mack winked when he added the candy to the order.

"No charge for candy for first time customers. I'll have Tom deliver this for you in about an hour. That OK? Want to take the candy with you?

"Sure! I will be back for more, but that is all I can think of now.

Back at the boarding house she sucked on the hard candy, reflecting on her new life.

Just then, young Tom raced into the boarding house, and dumped the supplies on the floor. He ran towards the door, but Mrs. Sullivan grabbed him by the collar. "What is the matter with you today? Where are your manners?"

"I gots to find Mr. Bill. Mrs. Colby is taken real sick. We gotta find the doctor."

Sarah heard Tom and hastened downstairs. "Is somebody sick?"

"Mrs. Colby has a sick heart and we gotta gets the doctor."

"Tell me where she lives. Maybe I can help."

Tom eyed her dubiously. Mrs. Sullivan directed, "She lives in the gray house on Fourth Street. Mrs. Colby is one of the prominent church woman a town."

Sarah raced to the house. What would she find? A heart attack in progress Heart failure? Knocking on the door of the gray house, a diminutive blonde woman answered.

Sarah asserted, "I am Dr. May. I am here to see Mrs. Colby." She felt like a total fraud. The maid escorted her to the bedroom. Mrs. Colby was large woman laying propped in bed, clearly in distress. Sweat beaded her forehead and she breathed with considerable effort. As Sarah reached, her Mrs. Colby turned her head, vomiting into a basin. Sarah grabbed a cotton towel dipped into water and wiped her mouth. She introduced herself, all the while patting cool water over Mrs. Colby's face and neck. "Tom told me your sick."

"I started feeling poorly about a week ago. Dr. Hancock came to see me but I feel worse. Is he going to come?"

"They are riding to find him. "What are your symptoms?"

"I am vomiting, as you can see. Look how swollen my ankles are." Sarah pulled back the covers. She pressed her finger into the swelling; it left a deep fingerprint.
"I am so weak I can hardly lift my hands."

"Has Dr. Hancock diagnosed you with any diseases?

"Yes, he says I have heart failure." Sarah would give her right arm for a stethoscope and blood Pressure cuff. She knew stethoscopes existed. Maybe Mack could order one. A thermometer, too. Blood pressure cuffs were not invented until later. Making do, she picked up Mrs. Colby's limp wrist, taking her pulse. Without a watch, she could only estimate, but thought the beats registered between 40-50 rather than more normal 80 beats per minute.

"Mrs. Colby, what medicines do you take?"
"Quinine, laudanum and digitalis." Bingo - digitalis. "How is your vision?"

"Blurry. It is so strange because everything looks green around the edges." Double - Bingo." Even with her limited diagnostic tools, Sarah felt sure that her patient suffered from an overdose of digitalis in her system. It could easily occur with patent medicines. In 2022, the sick woman would be hospitalized and given supportive treatment until her blood levels normalized. Out here, Sarah could only stop the medication, waiting until she recovered.

Her nursing side kicked in. The maid helped her change her nightgown and the linens. "Do you have any peppermint tea?" she asked the servant. In an hour Mrs. Colby lay in bed, sipping the tea. Her illness continued, but at least she lay comfortably. Sarah stayed the afternoon. Around 6, Dr. Hancock entered the room. Sarah remained in the background while he examined Mrs. Colby. "My dear, I think you are experiencing a bout of your heart failure. Clear liquids for three days, and bed rest for a week. Absolutely no salt. Take your medications as I prescribed. Your nurse can take care of you." He motioned to Sarah.
She jumped to her feet." Dr. Hancock, I would like to introduce myself. I am Dr. Sarah May. I am new in town."

He eyed her dress, not believing a word. Sarah pulled out the physician/missionary/father story again, glad that it fit another circumstance. "I have not finished my apprenticeship, so there are gaps in my training." Did you notice Mrs. Colby's heart rate?" she asked.

"I heard that it slowed some."
"Mrs. Colby told me she has nausea and vomiting as well as green halo vision."

"When did your father teach you about this halo vision ?" He distrusted her assessment.

"All these symptoms point to digitalis toxicity," she asserted.

"Oh, nonsense young lady. Our patient is experiencing an exacerbation of her heart failure."

"Is it possible that she used a new bottle of medicine mixed differently?"

Mrs. Colby piped up, "Remember Dr. Hancock? You gave me a fresh bottle a week ago."

Sarah could see a muscle jump in his jaw.

"Take all of your medicines. Just as I ordered. I will come back to see you in three or four days." He left.

Sarah worried that the digitalis poisoning would kill the woman. But she needed to build a relationship with the doctor. "I think we should follow your doctor's orders. But maybe you might forget to take the medicine for a few days? I'll come every day to make sure you are improving." Sarah knew Mrs. Colby's approval would be instrumental in establishing paying medical practice. She held her breath.

"You know doctor; I do get forgetful sometimes."

Sarah trudged back to the boarding house. Mrs. Sullivan said, "I kept a cold plate for you, honey. I don't usually do that for the girls, but since you are a doctor, you can't help being late." Sarah welcomed the consideration, eating every bite. "I will heat some bathing water for you if you refill the bucket Look for the water pump in the back,"

"A wash-up will be refreshing." Sarah took the bucket and found the pump. She stepped back to think through how to use the pump. Did it have to be primed? She vigorously pumped the water until the bucket filled and went Into the house, placing it on the stove. The cast iron stove sported multiple doors and plates. Sarah was dead sure she could not prepare a meal on it to save her soul.

"Could you put some wood in the stove? It is too cool to heat the water." Sarah found the kindling, then played Let's Make a Deal to figure out the correct door.

Taking her bath, she dressed in her nightgown to sit in her chair for a while. She wanted to light the kerosene lamp but had no idea how. Mia immediately filled the quiet. The cacophony of the day, kept Mia at bay, but the silence of the night brought her child into her arms. Tears flowed down her cheeks and her heart broke over and over again. Finally she went to bed and slept restlessly, until the sound of the other girls getting ready for breakfast woke her.

Her landlady's eyebrows furred when she saw Sarah. "Breakfast is at six."

"I'm sorry. I'll go to Mack's and buy an alarm clock today." Sarah looked at the group of young women around the table. She couldn't help but contrast breakfast at the brothel with breakfast here. The girls sat primly at the table ready for the day. The fashion seemed to be early Gibson girl. All were corseted into skirts made of colors more subdued than the de rigor of the brothel. Some wore white blouses with puffed Sleeves. Others wore modest bodices that closed at the neck and coordinated with the skirt. All had accents of lace, ruffles or bows. Sarah's sad calico seemed centuries old. Some girls looked at her poor calico dress in disdain.

Not much difference than the girls at the brothel.

Mrs. Sullivan sat, the girls folded their hands and bowed their heads in prayer. In respect to their religion, Sarah bent her head but kept her hands unclasped in her lap. Mrs. Sullivan frowned but began the prayer anyway.

"Amen," they chorused. Sarah looked up, putting a bright expression is her face.

Mrs. Sullivan led the introductions. "Sarah will be staying with us for a while. She recently lost her missionary parents."

"Ooh," said the girls in sympathetic unison.

"Sarah is a doctor and will be looking for new patients." That unexpected revelation stirred the girls. Mrs. Sullivan went on to introduce her other tenants. Miss Lark was the schoolteacher. She had kind eyes that welcomed Sarah. Miss Clarissa worked at the bank. She seemed to remember Sarah from yesterday. Another girl worked in the dress shop. The rest hired out a housemaids. The food was served in an orderly manner, always right to left, with a please and thank you. Polite conversation ensued.

"I heard the Polson twins had the measles."

"Yes, they will be out for at least a week. I will bring their work to them after school."

"Anything happen at the bank yesterday?" Sarah froze.

"Not a soul came in." Clarissa looked directly at Sarah.

A girl named Liza piped up. "You have such beautiful hair, Sarah."

"Thank you." Sarah self-consciously smoothed it back. The other girls styled their and pinned to their head, with strands and curls falling in all the right places.

"It would look nicer braided and pinned up." Sarah felt embarrassed perceiving a veiled insult. She was wrong, though.

"I can show you how to do your hair. I help all the girls." The women exclaimed about Liza's talent.

"Chiding herself for jumping to conclusions, she said, "I would love your help. For the first time, Sarah felt a little accepted in this old town.

"Is that the only dress you have?" Mrs. Sullivan asked. "Yes, but I bought fabric and notions to make two more dresses."

"What fabric did you buy?"

"A gold and green calico and a red plaid." "That will look nice with your eyes and hair. I would love to help. You know how I like sewing. I even have some patterns in the attic."

"That would be great! When can we start?" "After you buy that alarm clock!" Mrs. Sullivan laughed. Working with Mrs. Sullivan to choose the patterns began a friendship and camaraderie. "I noticed you do not wear a corset. All ladies in town wear one.

"My father forbid me from wearing them. He said corsets cause intestinal illnesses in women." This imaginary father helped bridge the century once again.

They finished cutting the dress fabric before Sarah left to go to Mack's, then visit Mrs. Colby. Her patient appeared a bit better. Sarah's new watch helped her determine her pulse was 55 now. An improvement, maybe it will be above 60 tomorrow. The new thermometer registered a normal temperature.

The two chatted amicably. Mrs. Colby pressed Sarah for more history. Sarah remained evasive, deftly changing the subject.

Stay or Go?

"Mrs. Sullivan says you hold important positions in the church."
That brightened her patient's mood. She described her various
leadership commitments in the strict Methodist church. "I hope
we can depend on you to join some of the committees once you
are settled." This expectation was going to be a real problem,
Sarah thought grimly. In addition, Mrs. Sullivan only rented to
good Christian ladies. After Sarah's loss of Mia, she would never
set foot in a church again. Christian churches in America
dictated societal behavior now as well as the future.

"I need to go home. Mrs. Sullivan and I are making new dresses.
This one is miserably used. I'll be back tomorrow."

Sarah did not know how to light the kerosene lantern. With
kerosene Combustible properties, asking was her only safe
choice. "Mrs. Sullivan your lantern looks different than the ones
we used. Can you show me head to light it?"

Her landlady paused, studying Sarah a bit. "Certainly, I'll be
happy to show you."

Sarah thought while sewing. She needed to be careful not to say
things like airplanes, highways, smart phones, or anything that
had not yet been invented. She knew some unexpected dialect
often came out by the way people cocked their heads at her. Not
having the ability to use everyday objects also made her suspect.
She needed to mimic their speech and actions.

Sarah's day seemed so busy that the thought of Mia was only a
light weight in her tattoo. Grief descended at night. She longed

for the arms of her little girl, wanting to smother her with kisses. Sarah cried herself to sleep each night.

Dr. Hancock was already treating Mrs. Colby when Sarah arrived. "I see our patient is much better. Her pulse is regular. Dr. Hancock looked directly at Sarah. Mrs. Colby told me she was also a little forgetful the past few days."

Uh-oh, here it comes.

"Excellent diagnosis doctor. It seems I was too hasty." Sarah exhaled a sigh of relief. Did you say you apprenticed under your father before he died?"

"I did."

I'm the only doctor for two towns and could use the help. I would like to offer you my services as a mentor."

"That would be wonderful! Thank you!"

We can spend time discussing cases. I'll loan you medical books. You can make rounds with me once or twice a month."

"That would work for me. But I do have one restriction. I am not interested in learning surgery right now. Maybe I could learn that a little further on."

"That's a good idea. There's much to do and much to learn. Refer the surgery cases to you me. Have you met Maddy yet?"

"No, I haven't."

"Maddy is the midwife in Jordan. She has birthed most of this town in the past 50 years. I wouldn't want you to take over for her. But I have a hunch if she like you, she will welcome help with prenatal and postnatal care. She is in her late 70's."

"I'll try to meet her this week."

"I think we have a deal then Dr. May." He reached out his hand, and Sarah shook it firmly.

A few days later, Sarah rode in Dr. Hancock's carriage as he conducted his rounds. She was nervous, worried that her ignorance of century old medical practices would, give her away. She kept a steady chatter of questions.

"What medications do you keep in your bag?"

"A country doctor like me does not have access to the variety of medicines available in the cities. But I keep the basics. Mack's stocks Munyon's remedies. Of course, Munyon's Homeopathies has a cure for everything – measles, tuberculosis, diarrhea, women's problems. Someone told me he has over 50 kinds of pills.
Sarah remembered seeing them in the store. Families usually call me if the pills don't work. Which they do not. I wish they would save their money."

The doctor steered the carriage to the front of the first house. "The baby has diarrhea that has been going on for a week. It is hard to save a little one after being sick so long." In the house,

Dr. Hancock examined the dehydrated child. "How often does he have diarrhea?"

"Maybe eight times a day. It is getting bloody now," whispered the worried mother.

"Can he drink?" asked Sarah.

"He drank some yesterday, but now he won't." Sarah felt panic at the baby's sunken eyes and wrinkled skin. She longed to pop an IV in to give life-saving intravenous fluids.

"Here is some opium. Give a teaspoon every two hours until the diarrhea stops," offered the doctor.

"Opium! Sarah wanted to cry out. But it would slow his bowel motility. What else was there? Try to wet a rag and dab some fluids is mouth. Make a weak solution of salt water." Dr. Hancock shrugged his shoulders at the unusual remedy, but said nothing as they left.

"He isn't going to live, is he?"

"No. I'm sure you know that there is a 20% mortality rate for infants with diarrhea." Sarah was secretly horrified.

The next visit they saw a man with his hand crushed in a steam engine belt. The hand swelled three times its normal size. It was clearly infected. Dr. Hancock let Sarah clean the wound. She first scrubbed her hands with a bar of strong lye soap from a bucket. It burned a little cut on her hand. After changing the dressing, she washed again.

"The infection has spread a little more. I will bleed you again."
The man's set his face in a resolute expression. Sarah pulled the
doctor to the corner whispering, "Have you seen the new studies
from back East?" They report that bloodletting has proved
ineffective."

"Nonsense, young lady, I see it work time and time again." He
performed the procedure. Sarah swore he let more blood than
usual to prove a point. Sarah washed her hands at the next few
houses. Dt Hancock remarked, "You are a fan of Dr. Lister, are
you?"

"I am. I am convinced that many diseases are spread from
germs."

"It doesn't hurt anybody, but it is a waste of time, in my
opinion."

"I wonder if you would consider washing your hands when you
care for children? They are so vulnerable?"

"I will think about it."

Sarah despaired as the day continued. Most remedies involved
morphine, heroin, or cocaine. The families firmly believed in the
powers of the store-bought medicines. By the time they called
the doctor, the patient's health was precarious. Sarah assisted
the doctor in some minor surgeries. She made a big to – do
about washing her hands. So much that the doctor was
obligated to do the same.

Besides the children, the tuberculosis patients wrenched her heart. There was no cure for the disease; close living quarters often infected the whole family. Sarah taught them about using handkerchiefs and spitting on the floor. Dr. Hancock encouraged them to move to a cold dry climate the Colorado. Their cavernous faces bowed they had no means to relocate.

Despite the overwhelming illnesses, Dr. Hancock met every patient with a smile. He knew the names of all the children, and who was related to whom. The families awaited his visits eagerly. Even the sickest of patients perked up because they felt hope had arrived.

"How do you do it?"

"Do what?"

"Keep up their spirits; give them hope."

Dr. Hancock pursed his lips. "Medicine is much more than making a diagnosis and administering medications. A person's spirit sustains a tremendous ability to heal their own body. I try to tap into that feeling with every patient I touch."

Dr. Hancock warned her about the last patient of the day, Mrs. Preston. "Mr. Preston went on a drunk last night, and I am afraid his wife is the worse for wear."

"What do you mean?"

"I heard he roughed her up pretty bad." They walked into the cabin and saw her lying in bed. Both eyes were blackened from the blows. Blood dried on her cheeks except for the areas where tears washed them clean. Three young children huddled in a corner.

"How are you holding up?" asked the gentle doctor.

"He cut into me right bad. He was pretty likkered up. Hit me in the face and I fell on the floor. Then he started kicking me right awful. I'm worried because I am peeing blood."

Sarah felt her head explode. "Your husband did this to you? Where is he? Has anybody called the sheriff?"

Mrs. Preston tried to look at her from under swollen lids. 'Why would the sheriff-come? No law will help me."

Dr. Hancock cleared his throat. "Sarah, it can be a terrible thing, but a man has authority over his wife. You know that."

"How do often does he beat you! Are the children there when he does it? He needs to be shot! Or at least jailed. You need to leave right away."

At that, the doctor jerked Sarah out of the home. "You are complete out of line, young lady. None of us like to see a woman suffer, but all we can do treat her when it happens. Some women can go back to their family. Mrs. Preston has no one. Ranting like that just adds to her suffering. If you can't keep your mouth shut, I'll not let you go back in there.

Rage coursed through her body. A few days ago, she was a whore without rights.   Now she realized she was a woman without rights.

For Christ's sake, women don't even get to vote for forty more years.

"Maybe I should get the children something to eat while you take care of Mrs. Preston." Sarah felt cowardly but knew she could not hold her tongue. Sarah avoided looking at the battered woman while the doctor tended to her. She found bread and jam then herded the children out into the yard, feeding them breakfast, lunch and almost dinner. They ate ravenously. They acted like they had witnessed this scene before. Thoughts flooded through her head.

Sarah was silent on the way home. How could she live here without legal rights? Marrying, she would come under the authority of a man. The situations was untenable. What would it be like in a world without antibiotics? A time with so little knowledge of the causes of disease? People recovered on the own. Some had extraordinary energy to heal the worst disease. Did she have the skill to help patients help themselves? Can I live in such a world? Live in a world that hurt and killed so easily?

Sarah compared today's patients with Mia. Dr. Patel read every new journal article on leukemia, authoring many of them herself. Mia received every medication and support system possible. But she died too. Was then really a difference between these two centuries?

In the modern world, women were supposedly protected against domestic violence. But were they really? Women were assaulted and killed regularly. It was still legal to beat your wife in many countries.

Immunizations and antibiotics were dispensed to children. Tuberculosis was not a death sentence. Children did not die of diarrhea – at least not in developed worlds. What about that? What did a mother in Sudan think when her son died of diarrhea that was easily curable in another part of the world? How could things be so much the same and so different? Sarah's head swam. She needed to choose a path. The 1880's was fraught with danger.

Curing Mrs. Colby launched her practice. It became fashionable to procure Sarah's services. Many women preferred a female doctor. Tom cheerfully produced her second case, with a broken arm. It was a simple fracture; she reset and placed a splint on it. She told him to keep the arm in the splint for a month but figured he would remove it within a week.

Sarah had an idea of another source of patients that would give her steady income. Plus ensure needed silence. Bolstered by her new dress and becoming hairdo, Sarah knocked on the door of Miss Ellie's boarding house. Kat opened the door, causing Sarah to step back. "I am here to see Miss Ellie."

Sarah had an idea of another source of patients that would give her a steady income. Plus, it would ensure needed silence.

Bolstered by her new dress and becoming hairdo, Sarah knocked on the door of Miss Ellie's boarding house. Kat opened the door, causing Sarah to step back.

"I am here to see Miss Ellie."

"Maybe Miss Ellie don't want to see you, accounting you up and left."

"Tell her I am here on business." Kat strolled to the back, and Miss Ellie came out of her office. Sarah could not read her face. "I have a business proposition for you,"

"What is that dear?"

"How much does Dr. Hancock charge you to check your girls for disease?"

"Why do you want to know?"

"I am looking to make money in this town as a doctor. Maybe we can help each other."

That got her interest. "He charges me $2 a girl. Overcharges me. He hates the job because he disapproves of our trade.

"I'll do it for $1.50 a girl."

Miss Ellie leaned against the doorway. "Why are you doing me a favor?"

"My second bill comes in the form of silence. I was never here."

"Silence will cost you fifty cents a girl."

"Forty sense and I would tell the town your girls have the clap."

Miss Ellis gave a belly laugh. "Honey, I like your style. Heck, I even like you, even if you did get up and leave."

"I paid my debt plus more.

"Yes, but I bet we won't see John hear anymore."

Sarah flush, not wanting to think about John.

Sarah kept busy over the next week, referred from one house to another. She encountered case after case of unfamiliar infectious diseases.

Time traveler Book heroines never had trouble remembering what they learned in nursing school. I don't remember a thing.

Vaccines could prevent the diseases. Antibiotics could cure most of them. Men and Women with caved in faces coughing blood probably had tuberculosis. They called Sarah when they couldn't breathe. Their disease was a death sentence. Sarah felt shocked at the extent of the illness throughout the population. She easily recognized the run of chickenpox, teaching mothers to keep the sores clean and to use oatmeal baths for the itching. She never saw measles before, so was relieved when a mother identified her son as having a case. She remembered measles as being highly contagious with frequent complications. Didn't Mary on Little House on the Prairie go blind because of measles? Sarah examined the child. His fever burned at 104 degrees. She excused herself to go Mack's to obtain extract of willow bark.

"Hi, Sarah!"

"I need extract of willow bark. Did any of my supplies come in?"

"I've got your medical bag, your stethoscope, rubber gloves and some splints."

"That will help." She gathered her supplies, turning to go back to the house.

She literally bumped into John. There he stood all hard and masculine, yet his eyes smiled softening his stance.

"I heard you are the doctor now"

"Just getting my feet wet."

Their hazel eyed gazes met. "I keep hanging around Mack's to see if I can run into you. Got lucky today."

"I want to stay and talk but I have a sick child."

"I'd be honored to be your driver." He untied his horse.

Sarah could not help but stare at its color. It was exactly the color of her hair. `What's her name?"

"Chestnut." He swung Sarah by the waist into the saddle. "Which way my dear?"

"Out to the Bingham farm."

Sarah suffered poor relationships with big four-legged creatures. She twisted and turned to get her seat. Her movement made Chestnut dance.

"What are you doing, haven't you ever ridden a horse?"

"Uh, no."

John settled her firmly against his lap as they trotted off. Sarah loved feeling his strong arms around her with his beard tickling her cheek. Every time Chestnut dropped her gait in her trot, Sarah's bottom bumped against John's lap. She should be humiliated, like in those romance novels, but instead wanted the ride to last forever. Apparently, John felt the same way. It wasn't hot outside, but they both were in a lather when they arrived.

"Thank goodness, one more mile and I would need to wash my pants."

Sarah laughed but slid down and ran into the house.

The toddler looked even sicker. Sarah measured out what she hoped would be the right dose of willow bark. Listening to his lungs with her new stethoscope. She heard no sign of pneumonia. The mother had closed the windows and drew the shades. There was not a breath of air in the room. Sarah made sure the child's eyes were covered from the painful light and opened the windows for fresh air. She instructed the mother, "Fresh air is good, as long as he doesn't get a chill."

Sarah showed her how to use cool cloths against his head, arms, and belly. "That will help with the fever." Sarah worried that giving the child as aspirin derivative would induce Reye's

Syndrome. But acetaminophen formulation lay in the future. Sarah's ministrations worked. The little boy's temperature dropped to 100 degrees.

"Is he going to be all right?"

"I think he will."

"Thank goodness; I don't think I could bear losing another one."

"How many have lost?"

"I've lost four. My little Robbie made it until almost two. He died of the fever. My baby died at six months to the day he was born of the bloody flux. I lost two before they was born."

In this intimate moment between women, Sarah shared her secret. "I lost my daughter Mia. She was 3 1/2. I still can't bear the pain. You have lost four. How did you get over it?"

"You ain't never get over it, Dr. Sarah. I pray to God every day to get me through."

But there is no God for me.

Sarah said goodbye and found John sitting under a tree with Chestier grazing near him.

"Is he going to be OK?"

She nodded.

"You look tired."

"I am. I spend my time walking from house to house, from farm to farm. I wish I could find a bicycle, that would be a big help."

"What is this bicycle? I'll try to get one for you."

Maybe they haven't been invented yet? "Uh, I think they only have them back East." "You need a horse." "I know I do, but..."

"But what?"

"I don't seem to get along with them."

"I have been wondering since I met you if you had fallen off a horse and hit your head."

"Ha-ha." Sarah wondered how this man could make her laugh so easily.

"Seriously, I could get you a horse and give you lessons."

Sarah arched her eyebrow.

" Not that kind of lesson, though I would throw that in for free."

It would give us a reason to be together.

Then, "I didn't know to make of the two gold pieces."

"It meant I wanted you to make the best possible life for yourself."

Sarah met John behind the livery for her first tiding lesson. Her borrowed riding pants were tight across her derriere, a fact not unnoticed by John. He trotted in with Chestnut. Another man rode a gray dappled horse.

"Let me introduce you to my partner in crime on the homestead - Bill Redd."

"I'm happy to meet you. John exaggerates; I am the hired hand. Besides, with John's reputation, I don't want to be thrown in the same lot with him."

"I don't blame you. I am beginning to feel the same way."

Bill dismounted, handing the reins to Sarah. Sarah looked skeptically at the horse. She peeked underneath its nether regions. "What is his name?"

"Clover," said John.

"Clover – that's what you would call a cow."

John shrugged his shoulders. "I asked him, and he said his name was Clover. Who am I to change his name?"

"So how did Chestnut get her name?"

"Did you see her coat is exactly the color of your hair? I told her how I loved her coat because my girl's hair was the same. So, I bought her. Before we rode off, I asked her name. She said Chestnut. So there you are."

Sarah rolled her eyes. "You think I look like a horse."

"My Faither said if you rolled your eyes back like that they would get stuck." All right, he had her there; she started laughing again.

"Show me how to ride Clover, the cow horse. Get it? Like cowboy?" He laughed and rolled his eyes.

128

John was sweating from the morning's work. His denim shirt sleeves were rolled to his elbows, and a couple of buttons opened at his chest. Dirt smudged one cheekbone. God, he never looked sexier.

"OK, Clover is the gentlest horse on the homestead. A baby could ride him." He showed Sarah how to groom and put the tack on her. "A livery boy will do this for you if you want. But you need to know how. Upsy-daisy." John held a hand for her foot.

She mounted gracefully on Clover.

Well, that was a first.

Now take the reins in one hand, nudge her with your heels and give a sound. She did, Clover moved, and Sarah immediately grabbed the saddle horn for safety.

"You are only walking, let go!"

Sarah shook her head.

"Ach, you are made of stronger stuff than that. Give her a kick and go. A small group of men came to the fence. At first, boredom attracted them. They watched Sarah grapple with the horse. She grabbed for the mane, clicked, and pulled on the reins, finally confusing the horse into a standstill. The loud guffaws made her turn pink.

Somehow steering Clover back over to the barn, she hissed, "Make them go away"!

"Honey, you are the most entertainment the boys will have today. You are lucky the whole town isn't here." Sarah sat straight in the saddle trying to remember John's instructions. She clicked Clover forward.

"Turn her right." Sarah confused Clover to the left. "The other right!"

The men laughed. John's smile widened, but he controlled his laughter. Clover, rather than Sarah, figured out the correct direction. "Kick her again." Clover was surprised into a trot. Not as surprised as Sarah who ended on the ground in two strides. Y

The men started murmuring. It looked like money changed hands. John strode over. "OK, up you go."

Sarah started to protest, but he interrupted. "Once you fall off a horse you get right back in the saddle."

Sarah found herself atop poor Clover again. John directed an attempt into figure eights. Near the men, Clover turned into the fence.

Damn.

She thought the curse word was under her breath. Wrong – it could be heard as clear as a bell. She didn't complete another circuit before Clover backed up, instead of going forward.

Shit.

The men started exchanging money with alacrity.

"What are they doing?"

"Betting on how many curse words you will say."

"Oh."

"I dare you to go out there and make them blush."

"Hardly, I am trying to establish a reputation as a lady."

"Double dog dare you." Sarah stopped protesting and seemed to think about it for a second.

Cupping his hand to her ear, he said, "Triple dog dare you."

Sarah moved Clover back into the ring. She didn't have to fake a mistake. At the midpoint of the corral, the horse felt he had enough and stopped dead. No amount of kicking or clicking moved him. She proceeded to spar a protracted string of expletives that caused a few of the men to truly bluest.

Sliding off the horse, she strolled to the fence collecting every dollar that had been bet against her. "Thank you, gentlemen," smiling her wide grin. It paid to be around a motorcycle gang.

John and Bill in the barn, laughed as tears ran down their faces. "It's not hard to make money in this town," she said archly.

John walked her home. About halfway, hip cramps started.

"Ah- ah-ah!"

"It does kinda hurt first, but you will get used to it."

"I feel like my hips and my bottom have been whipped."

"Ach, I would love to soothe those wee little aches and pains for you," he breathed in her ear.

Ach, I wish you would.

After two lessons, John took Sarah to the path that circled the town. In spite of the frequent traffic, they could talk quietly together. Chester pranced along with John riding in rhythm. Clover clomped along while Sarah tried to relax in the saddle. The sun shone against the blue sky, emptied of clouds. John took the lead when the path narrowed. Sarah watched the muscles in his back flex rhythmically with Chestnut's gait. She appreciated the outline of his work-hardened biceps. The trail widened and John slowed down. Sarah came abreast, her heart skipping more than one beats ashis handsome lightly bearded face came into view. It unsettled her to see her eves on his face.

"How is Dr. Sarah's practice progressing?"

"I am on the right track. I have arranged with Dr. Hancock to continue my apprenticeship. I spend my days traveling from patient to patient, hopefully providing correct treatments.

"Are you happy."

Sarah was taken aback. When is the last time had she been asked that question?

"Are you happy being a doctor in a small town?"

"I don't know yet. There hasn't been enough time. People are sick with illnesses I don't normally see. I'm not familiar with some of the remedies."

"Like what?'

Stay or Go?

"We sometimes administer shots instead of oral medicine. "Sarah could tell by John's expression he thought she was being evasive,

"Have you found a barrister to help you?"

"No luck. Barrister's don't work after hours and homesteaders don't study during the day."

"I accomplished something important today."

"What was that?" Sarah told him about her relationship with Miss Ellie.

"That's great, With your secret safe, we can officially court."

"What does courting involve, specifically."

"I pick you up, dressed like a slick cowboy in my open carriage. Mrs. Sullivan stands on the porch and looks stern. She will admonish you to be back by dark, or your reputation will be ruined".

"So, what does courting really involve?"

"I take a bath and generally won't smell like a horse. I comb my hair. Maybe trim my beard if I have the time. I'll ride Chester and bring Clover since I don't own a carriage. I'll sincerely agree to Mrs. Sullivan's rules. Then I will coax you away from the trail to a secluded spot."

"Then I will pull the ribbon out of your hair letting it fall on your shoulders. I will comb my fingers in your curls, I'll pull you close and kiss every one of your freckles. He cocked his head and looked at her face. That may take a while, but that is OK."

"Is that all?"

"Och, I'll be too tired to do anything else."

She shot him a dirty look.

"Besides, I have something more important."

"What's that?"

"Tell me more about you."

A touchy topic. I seemed Sarah could lie to every person in this town, but John was different. She could not lie to him. What would she tell him? About being Mike's wife and Mia's mother? Even before that, a girl who loved the outdoors and mountains? When did she give that up? When she got on the motorcycle? Could she regain her true self in this lifetime?

"I'll tell you what I like. I love going to the mountains. I take in the colors- verdant grass, the gray granite of the mountain tops, the turquoise lakes if I can find them. I wrap my arms around jack pines and breathe in their smell of vanilla. If I can get the birds to them, I adore those tiny red strawberries. Two little berries burst with more flavor than a whole garden of cultivated ones. I am at peace sitting on a rock with a Breeze blowing through my hair, feeling like I know this rock from another lifetime.

"You are a rare woman Sarah May."

As they rounded the corner, John broke into a cowboy song. Sarah felt a little embarrassed, it realized everybody sang out loud this century. On the third verse, he waited for Sarah to chime in, but she remained silent.

"Sing!"

"I don't know that song very well."

"Everybody knows this song."

John taught it to her and soon they were singing full out riding down the road. Passersby tipped their hats to the performance.

"OK, your turn to sing a song."

"Oh, I don't know a good song."

She knew no century-old songs. It would have to be a modern one.

"I see leaves of green, red roses, too. I see them bloom for me and you..." Sarah thought Louis Armstrong was always appropriate.

Johnny was still when the song concluded he sat very still. "I have never heard a song like that. Is it part of you that is different?"

"It is one part of me."

"Can you tell me lass? Did you come from another city? What is such a deep secret?"

"Tears came to her eyes, but she said," I cannae say."

They came to Mrs. Sullivan's. He helped her dismount and Sarah felt him hold her tight as she slide down her body. Mrs. Sullivan stood on the porch with her arms crossed, preventing Sarah from receiving what she really wanted—a kiss.

Sarah thought of every excuse to tell Mrs. Sullivan about skipping church. The first Sunday she arrived, she was too tired. The second Sunday she had her period and couldn't leave her bed. The third Sunday came. Mrs. Sullivan tapped her foot impatiently.

"Wasn't your father a missionary? Did he believe in worshipping the Lord on Sundays?"

"He did."

"All of my girls attend church on Sunday and you are no exception."

Sarah bought herself another week by exposure to measles. Now she was out of excuses and out of time. Afterwards, she would have traded all the Sundays in a year to prevent what lay ahead.

Sarah met Maddy, the midwife. Though in her late 70's she was as spry as women half her age.

"Would you help me if I need a second pair of hands during a delivery?"

"That would be great," said Sarah, thinking of the learning opportunities.

On a Saturday evening, Maddy sent Tom for Sarah" help. Tying Clover at the house's post, she heard a moan, first low, then gaining strength, and then rip into a primal scream. Sarah froze, her fear rising.

I don't know nothing about birthing no babies, Miss Scarlet,

Ran through her mind.

Maddy saw outside of the window. "I'm glad you are here, hurry.

"Beatrice, this Sarah." Beatrice opened her eyes but hadn't the strength to talk.

"How long has she been in labor?"

"Going on twenty hours. Her water broke and it started right away. The baby is breech. I have tried everything I know to turn it. Beatrice has a narrow pelvis, and I don't know how this is going to turn out."

"Where is Dr. Hancock?"

"Two towns over with his own difficult delivery."

Maddy had given her all the laudanum she dared. Sarah helped Beatrice in every way she knew to ease her pain. Beatrice screamed in agony with every contraction. Maddy checked her cervix. "The cervix can't open with some breech babies, " gritted Maddy. They worked hour by hour into the night. Beatrice was exhausted, they worked to keep her awake. The hot room filled with the smell of blood.

In the middle of the night, Maddy checked her cervix again. Sarah knew something was very wrong. "The cord is hanging down." The umbilical cord cut off the mother's blood flow to the baby. A breech baby with a blocked umbilical cord was death sentence. Sarah began suffering with the memory the of Mia's death. Maddy said, "Don't you go soft on me. Beatrice, the baby, and I all need you."

Sarah folded her emotions back in her heart. By morning, hope was gone. Beatrice pushed the baby's body out then fell unconscious for the last time. Blood flowed out of her. Nothing more could be done than hold the dying woman's hand. Maddy prayed.

On the way home on top of Clover, Sarah shivered until her teeth chattered. She began to cry, then keen convulsively. The event traumatized her. Sarah vowed she would never have a baby in such a barbaric environment.

How hard did Beatrice's husband pray for his wife and their child? No one listened to him either.

A week later, Sarah hung out at Mack's. She kept an ear out for John while playing checkers with Mack. The last time she played was as a ten-year-old girl. It showed when Mack beat her in 8 moves. "Hain't anybody ever taught you to play checkers, Dr. Sarah?"

"Obviously not."

"Good thing you are a better doctor than checker player. Lemme teach ya."

Just then, Chestnut trotted pass the door. "Oh, I have to go. Let's get back to lessons another day."

Mack noticed Chestnut as well as John. He chuckled as she ran out the door.

Sarah caught up with John as he was going into the livery. "John," she whispered. He turned his head and he lit up with his handsome smile.

Ach, you are a sight for sore eyes. Oh no, I don't have time to teach you a new song.

"This is serious. I need help." John became all business. "I have been putting Mrs. Sullivan off about going to church for a month. I can't put her off any longer. She might throw me out of the boarding house,"

"You've worked too hard to lose your reputation now. Why don't you just go to church?"

Sarah took in a deep breath. "I can't tell you why I won't go to church. I haven't done anything wrong, but I will never step foot in a church again. Never, I don't know what to do." Sarah took a step closer, and John could see the top of the calligraphy M on her neck.

"I'll trust you. The answer is easy. Tell her you are a Quaker. My Faither was a Quaker, and I am, too."

"I don't even know what being a Quaker means."

"Quakers do not have traditional church services. Some may have buildings some don't. We sit quietly and contemplate God in our heart. Sometimes a member speaks his heart, but usually it is a silent service."

"Is it Christian?"

"It is anything you want it to be. Do you think you could go to a Quaker service?"

"I'd try it."

"Go on home and tell Mrs. Sullivan that you are Quaker and are going to a service with me on Sunday. I'll pick you up at 8:00." She turned to leave.

"Don't wear your Sunday best, just wear something comfortable."

Mrs. Sullivan's eves narrowed in suspicion when learning of Sarah's church plans. "Why didn't you tell me you were a Quaker?"

"I didn't know if but there were other Quakers to worship with." Lame answer but better than no than no answer.

Eight o'clock sharp found John and Chestnut trotting to the boarding house. "Good day Mrs. Sullivan, you look resplendent in your church clothes.

"I suppose you are here to escort Dr. Sarah to church?"

"Yes ma'am I am. Would you consider accompanying us to our church this morning? You would contribute substantially to our service."

Flattered by John's sincere charm, she said, "Thank you for your offer, but I haven't ridden a horse since I was a little girl." They laughed at the picture.

Sarah watched the exchange. John wore his Sunday best courting clothes. He dressed in new blue jeans. A white crisply starched shirt matched his white teeth and that sexy smile. Add the trimmed beard and twinkling eyes, it was all Sarah could do not to run down and kiss him.

John enjoyed the scenery, too. Her riding pants emphasized all of the right places of her curves. Liza had braided her hair with strands of curls, whisking around her face. John's heart lurched seeing her broad smile. "Are we ready?" Sarah mounted Clover, and off they rode.

"My last is most beautiful this morning."

"My lad is a handsome Prince Charming."

"Who?"

"Never mind."

The couple laughed and talked on the trail. The ride seemed long. "I assume this Shaker meeting is not in a building."

"No, it is an unusual spot. Trust me." Soon they turned to a trail that led into a canyon.

"John, surely the meeting place isn't here."

"I swear to you it is" He dismounted Chester after crossing a small creek. "Here we are."

"Here we are what?"

"This is our meeting spot."

141

"Where are the others," asked Sarah suspiciously.

"I guess they didn't come today."

He held Sarah's hand, leading her a bit further. The view struck her silent. Twelve foot flat boulders were the lips of a waterfall. Clear water flowed over the edge, turning into. Burning white water before landing in a swirling turquoise pool, mesmerizing Sarah. John's heat radiated close behind her.

"No well me this isn't a meeting place. She nodded. He grasped her hand firmly, stone hopping to the other side of the creek. Sarah's usual clumsiness had her teetering on the edge of a slippery rock, but John held her steady.

"How did you find this place?"

"It found me one year." Now we will have our service. "Find a comfortable place to sit. He enunciated the next words. "Look at the innermost light in your heart.

"That's it?"

"It's harder than it looks."

Sarah sat with her feet hanging over the edge of the pool. John placed a mall Bible on a stone. "This is for me; in case I need it." He closed his eyes.

Sarah looked below, watching the circling water.

Look at the innermost light in my heart.

The pool drew her away from distractions. There was only the sound of the water, the circling pool and Sarah. Her tattoo tingled. Out of the light cam Mia. Mia as a bald baby with a toothless smile. Mia with her blonde curls and laughing smile. Total love, boxed in these month, emanated from her heart. Scenes from Mia's childhood poured into her consciousness. Sarah immersed herself, once again, into motherhood. The turquoise pool applied balm over her pain. Sarah felt the sarcophagus around her heart chip into little pieces. With the wall breached, healing began.

Hush little baby, don't say a word.....

Mamma's gonna buy you a mocking bird.....

She sang their song, with peace for the first time, then opened her eyes.

John tilted his head as she looked up. "You were singing. It sounded like a lullaby. Did you sing for a baby?"

Sarah thought for a moment. Sharing about Mia would not give away the core of her secret. She wanted to tell John about her child. John wrapped his arms around her shoulders.

"M" is for Mia. The name means beloved, my beloved daughter. She died a few months ago.

Sarah shared the love, joy and enchantment of Mia. She told anecdotes that made them laugh. She related stories of Mia growing from an infant to a precocious three year old. The details shortened. Mike leaving. Mia sick with a blood disease. Sarah

singing their song as Mia died. John wiped tears from his face.
He felt surprised that Sarah had none. "This is a sacred place."

"You can tell me anything. I cannot imagine there is anything
about you that would change that. This time Sarah's eyes welled
up.

They sat, basking in the sun with the light breeze blowing through
Sarah's curls. "Sing me that beautiful song."

"I see trees of green, red roses, too..."

John turned his head, gazing at Sarah after the last "oh yeah."
How do you know a song like that? Sarah didn't answer.

Let me tell you a story. This time Sarah looked up at him. "My
Faither loved my Ma with all his heart. He never considered
getting remarried after she died. Do you know what he told me?
Sarah shook her head. "He said he knew he was going to marry
her the minute he laid eyes on her. True love at first sight. Do
you believe in love at first sight, Sarah?" Sarah thought back to
that first night at Miss Ellie's. Those hazel eyes. John picked a
pink wild rose and held it out to Sarah.

John loves a woman, oh so rare,

Her smile, freckled face and chestnut hair.

Her hazel eyes,

Like mine, surprise,

Will you wed me

Sarah fair.

"Yes!, I mean no. Yes, but I can't!"

"But what does that mean? Do you not love me?"

"Yes, I love you. I am not sure you want to marry me."

"Of course, I want to marry you. I wouldn't have stayed awake all night writing that proposal if I wasn't sure."

"But you don't know about me. About my past life."

"Sarah I will love you no matter what you tell me."

"I am afraid if I tell you, I will lose you. If I don't tell you I can't marry you, and I will lose you,"

"Sarah, you are not making any sense."

"I have to choose between love and loss."

"That's an easy answer, Sarah."

"Not in this case. John, I love you, I want to marry you. Please give me a week to figure out what to do and how to do it."

"Sarah, please stay, do not go."

Straddling Time

Sarah arrived at Miss Ellie's at the appointed time. An unknown girl showed her in. Sarah knew how to identify the different sexually transmitted diseases from one of the books Dr. Hancock loaned her. She came prepared with plenty of rubber gloves, soap, and alcohol disinfectant. The girl said flatly, "the gals are in their rooms." Sarah trudged the familiar stair, glad to be free of this terrible life.

Thank you, John.

She progressed from room to room. So far, all the girls were clean. Knocking on the last door; she found Kat. "You ain't gonna touch me. You ain't a real doctor."

Sarah did not want to argue. Leaving the room, she said, "Fine. When I give my report to Miss Ellie, I will tell her that you deferred the exam."

"Git in here. If I don't get the test, Miss Ellie will kick me out." Sarah began the examination, her heart dropping. Obvious signs of gonorrhea were evident. "Does it hurt when you urinate?"

"When I what?"

Does it hurt when you pee?

"No." Sarah didn't believe her based on how swollen her urethra looked. Pressing on her abdomen, Kat's pain showed clearly on her face.

"I think you have the clap", using a term that Kat would understand.

"Think?

"I know you the clap."

Kat's temper burst, and she raged at Sarah.

"You are trying to get back at me. I'll tell you something. Your
      boyfriend sneaks back every night. We laugh at you. If I
      have the clap, then so do you " Kat pushed towards her.
      Sarah made haste out the door. Kat trailed two steps
      behind. Both screeched to a halt when Miss Ellie
      appeared, hands crossed over her large bosom.

"Ladies"

"That fake doctor says I have the clap, but I don't. She's jes'
      trying to get back at me."

"Sarah?"

"Kat shows clear signs of gonorrhea. I recommend stopping her
trade to go to town for treatment.

"It ain't true," squalled Kat.

"My job is to check the girls and give you my recommendations.
If a customer asks me how he got gonorrhea, I will tell him the
truth. You have a reputation for a clean house. I know you want
to keep it that way."

Miss Ellie hedged but decided to take Sarah's advice.

Kat scared Sarah. "Miss Ellie, I will not be threatened. She
grabbed her bag and headed for the door. Before leaving,
something occurred to her, "Where is Adele?"

"I asked Adele to leave."

"Leave, why?"

"She got sick too many times. I wouldn't tolerate it. Sarah knew why Adele couldn't stay well. The treatment consisted of a poisonous mercury ointment that worked poorly, if at all. Also, Adele's low standing in the hierarchy of girls relegated the less desirable customers to her bed.

"Where is she?"

"I have no idea. probably set herself up in a crib by the railroad."

"What is a crib?"

"A little shack with a bed. Railroad me come in and jump all the girls they can for 50 cents each. If a girl is lucky, she might get twenty men a day.

Sarah backed up against a wall. "How long was that?"

"I don't know, maybe a week?"

"How can you do that to these girls?" asked Sarah angrily.

"What am I supposed to do, open a rest home for whores?"

Sarah mounted Clover. She kicked and cursed Clover into a fast trot. She found John fencing in an outer field.

"John, John! Please help me!"

"What's the matter?" looking her over for bodily injuries.

"Not me, it's Adele.

John's registered blankly.

"The sweet young girl at Miss Ellie's. Miss Ellie kicked her out last week. She started a crib by the railroad." John's paled at the news. "We have to find her."

"OK, " he thought. Chestnut can't carry all three of us. Clover canters slow, if at all. You are going to have to ride a faster horse. Do you think you can stay on one?"

Sarah would do whatever it took to save Adele. They saddled the horses. Sarah's horse sensed her panic and danced sideways. Sarah grabbed the horn, and, and anything she could hold. "Take the reins and pull him in hard," John instructed "Stop thinking about Adele and show the horse who is the boss." Sarah determined to rescue Adele straightened out the horse. They flew to the railroad.

It wasn't hard to find the cribs. A long line of dismal, shanties leaned near the empty railroad tracks. John helped Sarah dismount. Running to the first shack, a woman sat on a filthy mattress on the dirt floor. The acrid smell of unwashed flesh filled their nostrils. Sarah shrank back against John.

"Do you know Adele? Do you know which shanty is hers?"

The defeated woman looked at the two. "I don't know no Adele. These girls come and go. No use asking their names."

"Where do they go if they aren't here?"

"They go as low as they can go. They walk the streets, or kill themselves with liquor or opium."

Sarah thought, "How can this happen? What happens to a woman that makes a spiral done this path? But she couldn't help but think about the drugged homeless, back in her century.

"Is there anybody who might know?" "I dunno." John a wad of bills onto her mattress. She looked up for the first time. "You wanna make a go of it handsome?"

"No, that's for your help."

The woman brightened. "That's a lot of money for help."

The couple divided the cribs, looking into each one of them. Their calls of "Adele" were met with shouts of "Shut up!" or other obscene remarks.

Finally, Sarah saw the familiar face. "Adele! I have been looking all over for you." Adele sat up. Sarah winced at the fresh bruises on her face.

"Dr. Sarah? Am I dreaming?"

"No, John and I have come to take you home."

"I don't have a home anymore."

" I'm going to find you a safe place to live," Sarah promised.

" Oh, thank Mother Mary. I don't think I could stand it anymore.

John grabbed a blanket off Chestnut, cradled Adele protectively in his arms, and rode towards home. "Where are we going to take her? The hotel won't have her."

"I think I am going to find out how Christian Mrs. Sullivan is."

They rode to the boarding house and stood a wobbly Adele on her feet. Mrs. Sullivan rushed out the door. "Is she hurt? Did something happen?" The landlady stopped, recognizing Adele. "Sarah, you are not going to bring that, that thing into this house."

"This thing happens to be a sweet young girl who fell into terrible circumstances."

"She is a whore."

"She is a human being who needs help."

"I am a Christian woman, and whores cannot stay here." She quoted from the Bible:

"The woman must be taken to the door of her father's home, and there the men of her this tow must stone her to death, for she has committed a disgraceful crime in Israel by being promiscuous."

"Didn't Jesus say something like, *"What you did to one of the least of these children you did to me?"* Mrs. Sullivan crossed her arms. Adele swayed precariously, even as John held her. "You are a good

Christian woman," Sarah pleaded. "I could never win a battle of God's verses with you. I keep one Bible verse in my heart.

Do unto others as you would have them do unto you.

At that, Mrs. Sullivan's eyes teared. "Put her in the basement room, but only for a week". John carried Adele downstairs and laid her on the bed.

"I can take care of things now."

"Will I still see you Sunday?"

Sarah smiled. "How could I miss a date with my knight in shining armor?"

"Who?"

"No matter."

John leaned over and captured a kiss. "You are an incredible woman."

Sarah spent the rest of the morning nursing Adele, bathing her wounds, and giving her water. When Adele could tolerate water, Sarah walked to the kitchen to find her landlady warming broth on the stove.

"Thank you for what you have done, Mrs. Sullivan."

"I cannot refuse a woman in need. But Sarah, not everybody thinks this way. I will honor our three-month lease, but I will not renew it. I can't have you putting my reputation at risk." Sarah nodded her understanding.

"Would your church or Mrs. Colby know if there is a place where women like Adele can stay and be healed? Would you talk to her and join us in this ministry?"

Mrs. Sullivan reluctantly agreed. Sarah sighed in relief. Three days later Adele rode in a carriage toward the Convent of Mercy where she could be healed physically and spiritually.

Sarah's deadline with John arrived before the week's deadline. Dr. Hancock arrived in town, his horse wet with lather. "Sarah! A diphtheria outbreak has started. You need to watch for cases. It seems to be a particularly virulent form. Three children have died already."

Diphtheria, what did she know about diphtheria? Her mind was blank. A thick coating on the throat causing the child to suffocate. A race on a dogsled to deliver anti-toxin to an Alaskan village, now called the Iditarod." she fished, it knowing what treatments existed in the first place.

"None, this is a terrible disease. This form kills children in two to three days.

Sarah didn't have to tell the community to isolate. Mothers feared the disease and closed their families into their houses.

Sarah's first call was for three-year-old Mary. She lay in her mother's arms, breathing with a loud croup. Sarah ascertained the illness by inspecting the thick gray mucous in the back of the child's throat. Her fever was 102 degrees. When Sarah listened to her chest with her stethoscope, it sounded like a washing machine. "It's diphtheria. How long has she been sick?"

"It started yesterday. I didn't worry about it, but she is so much worse today." Three older children hovered in the room, worried about their sister.

"Don't let the other children come near Mary; keep them out of the house if you can." The frightened children left.

Sarah instructed the father to put a kettle on the stove to add humidity to the room. She tried to give Mary a tincture of willow bark, but the child could not swallow. What could be done to make her more comfortable? Antitoxin! She would give her soul to give Mary the cure for this disease. How did the population live before this lifesaving drug? The children did not. They died.

Mary's condition worsened. Her chest began to heave in respiratory distress as her airway closed.

She needs a tracheostomy.

"Do you have a pocket-knife?" She asked the father. He produced one from his pocket. "I also need a hollow tube about this big." The man dashed out the door and came back with a pipe. Sarah positioned Mary so that her throat was accessible. She knew the anatomy and the concept, but not the procedure. Think, think, she berated herself. Then a flash of memory came. Father Mulcahy performed a tracheotomy in the field on MASH. Why did my most helpful medical knowledge come from television and movies? Remembering Hawkeye's, the knife cut into the child's flesh. As the trachea opened, she slipped the tube in. Mary's respirations eased.

Sarah held the tube in place with the child on her lap. Mary struggled to breathe again. The pipe clogged from the copious thick secretions from the girl's lungs.

Oh, God no suction! Wiggling and turning the tube did not help. Mary once again struggled for every breath.

Her parent began grieving the inevitable. Mary slipped away before Sarah's eyes. A little girl wandered into the bedroom. "Mommy, I have a sore throat. Sarah handed Mary's body to her father.

"No more. Children are not going to die when there is another way."

Tommy had lingered in the streets after the school closed. Sarah called to him, "Tommy, get John and tell him to bring four of his best horses. Hurray! Ride as fast as you can." She slapped his horse and Tommy took off. Back at the boarding house, Sarah unrolled her 21st-century clothes. Her iPhone fell out. It had a 72% charge. This might be the proof she needed. Mrs. Sullivan frowned as Sarah waited impatiently for John. "I know this is strange, but I can help the children."

John and his horses thundered up the street. "Take me to Penrose Trail". He didn't question her, and they rode hard.

Stay or Go?

After dismounting Sarah said, "I desperately need your help. A black diphtheria epidemic has started."

"Oh my God, I will help any way I can."

"The first thing is that you have to believe me. I am going to tell you why I am different. When I am done, you do not have to love me, you do not have to marry me, but I need you to trust me for one thing."

John waited.

Sarah spoke distinctly. "I am from the future."

John shook his head; sure he didn't hear correctly.

"I didn't come here on purpose. I hiked to the Lost Twin Lakes with the intent of killing myself. I could not bear Mia's death.

"It is impossible to come from the future."

"I thought it was impossible, too, except here I am. I was ready to pull the trigger when an Indian woman White Buffalo showed me an archway. She told me I might find another path. I decided to try. When I came down the mountain it was 1882.

John's silent expression didn't change.

"I need to go back through the archway. We have medicines, wonderful medicines that can save the lives of our children. I want to go through the archway again to bring the medicines here.

"I don't know what to think."

She handed him the phone. "This might help you believe me. John looked at the object, turning it around. " It is called a smartphone. Most people have them in the future. It does many things. You can push a few buttons and talk to anybody on the planet. Another set of buttons function like a massive encyclopedia. You have the knowledge of the world at your fingertips. Even law books. Sarah turned it on, and the screen lit up. John fumbled with the phone. Some things won't work because we are in the past. I know one thing that will work. Sarah found the music app. Louis Armstrong's voice sang out his signature song.

John's demeanor changed. "I don't understand any of this, but I will trust you. One question? What is this smartphone made of?"

"Plastic. It is man-made and can be soft or hard, strong or weak, and can be formed into any shape and color. I need to ride to the archway. I need you to wait for me while I get the medicine. We can load the horses and ride back to town. Hopefully, I can cure most of the children."

"How do you know this archway will be there?"

"White Buffalo told me it would stay open if I had clear intent, but she didn't say how long. I should be back tomorrow night. The children can't wait much longer.

"What if you dinnae want to cum back to me? With your faincy life and all?"

Sarah threw herself into his arms. "I will move heaven and earth to get back to you. I also will move heaven and earth to get back to the children. I will be back to marry you if you will still have me. If you are going to help me, we need to make tracks."

"Make tracks?"

"It means hurry."

The horses needed water halfway up. "Tell me more."

How do you tell someone about the world?

"Let me start by saying what is the same. People. People are the same. There are proper church women, there are prostitutes. Babies are born and grow up. They die, too. People are kind and cruel and parsimonious. There are many more poor than rich. People of all races live together, yet there is terrible bigotry."

"What did you do?"

"I was a wife, a mother, and a nurse."

"You are not a doctor, then."

"Nurses know so much more in the future. There are many medical advances that nurses do. Just like the drugs I am getting. I thought that I could practice here, but all of the infectious diseases surprised me. We have something called antibiotics that cures many of them. The bloody flux kills so many now but can be cured with a couple of pills.

"What would I be if I were in the future?"

"You could be a lawyer. Or a rancher. Or anything you wanted to be.

Another hour brought them to the straggle of trees. Dismounting, Sarah stood at the side of her mount, not sure what John was thinking. He enfolded her in his arms. "I hope ye coom back; I dinnae know what I would do without ye."

"If I am not back in three days, something happened, and I can't get back." Sarah left the iPhone with John. She walked through the transparent archway. John's image disappeared.

John's head reeled. People did not drop in from the future. It was impossible. Maybe he caught diphtheria and was disoriented from a fever. Sarah, however, was very real. She was, somehow, always off just a bit. Her speech sounded a little odd, accented by a strange cadence. She was clumsy in the way she handles familiar objects. He remembered one hesitation when she talked about going to Scotland. She said "flew" and then corrected it to sailed. Odd. Can people fly in the future?

John settled the horses down. Sarah had disappeared through a narrow opening, but he could walk four horses for water in the same place. He sat with his back against a comfortable tree, looking at the plastic object. He gently tapped it on a rock. It was hard, but he thought he could break it with more force. The color looked glass-like, yet the material looked different. The front was dark. He brushed his thumb over a protrusion, lighting the contraption. Turning it around he could not find the source of illumination. John felt visually overheated by the light and color of the electronic screen. What the hell? He tried to make

160

sense of it and could see rounded squares with names or symbols. Google? What is a Google? He touched the button and was rewarded with a larger white screen. He explored various parts of the pictures. When he touched the box, a display of letters appeared. Surprised, he typed the letters 'Sarah then touched the curious arrow at the end. The box changed again, but only said 'No Internet Service." He tried other buttons with the same results. Where was the music? His eye caught on the button that said 'calculator'. The screen opened into familiar numbers and calculations. He typed 2+2=. The top of the screen immediately flashed '4'. He shrugged at the elementary math. Next, he typed 12 x 12=. '144' glowed on the screen. Let's try something harder. '150 divided by 36. '4,16666666667'. No one could do math like this; it could be calculated....in the future?

John began pushing every button he could find. He almost missed the one that said 'email'. He knew what mail meant, though as much as he wanted to see the secrets he held, he was too honorable to read Sarah's private correspondence.

Finally, he found a button which yielded the music. He readjusted against the tree, and closed his eyes, listening to melodies, harmonies, and rhythms that were not from his world. Some he liked, one he hated, and some made him want to dance in unfamiliar movements. Well after midnight he decided to sleep. As he put the smartphone down, he noticed a button he had missed. It said Calendar. John pressed it with trepidation. The date glared June 11, 2022. John stared into the darkness. As the sun set, he accepted that the woman he loved was indeed 140 years old.

Sarah felt relief after she cleared the archway. Her non-existent paddling skills drew the canoe in one direction, then the other. She heard jewel-like laughter. At its source stood White Buffalo and the children. Sarah weathered the teasing pretty well, after amusing most of the party.

"White Buffalo? Is this the right path?"

"If you ever get that canoe straight, your way is strong."

Great, even Indian spirits make fun of me.

Sarah flew down the mountain. She repeated the detailed list of supplies over and over in her mind. First, of course, the antitoxin. Additionally, antibiotics and medical necessities that where needed to treat a town for some time to come. The trail turned into pavement. Sarah ran to a popular stretch, sticking out her thumb. A friendly woman stopped. Sarah casually asked the date to reassure herself that the archway had transported her to the correct time. She needed Jane. Jane knew what had to be done. But did she trust a 140-year-old letter? Thanking the woman for the ride, she entered Jane's husband's pharmacy.

"Where's Jane!" and "There you are!" came out simultaneously. They embraced in relief.

"Did you get my letter?"

"Yes, we have everything ready for you. At first, I did not understand where you went. I looked for you for a month. I even filed a Missing Person's report. When I got the old letter, I didn't know what to think. I showed it to Joe. We read it over and over. Without the story about Thumper, we wouldn't have believed it. We decided to pack the things.

"Can I see the letter?"

Dear Jane,
I know you are worried about me. I am sorry, there was no way to communicate. I am safe and well. But I need your help.

My town possesses no medical supplies. There is a diphtheria outbreak, and I need antitoxin. While I am here, I want to purchase other supplies on the list. If you think of anything else, add it in. I'll need some pack horses. There are so many sick children. I will need to pack and leave right away.

Just so you know it is me, remember the story you told me about taking a scalpel to Thumper?
I will see you on June 12, 2022.

All my love,
Sarah

The letter was written on yellowed Wells Fargo paper stationery dated June 10, 1882. "Did you have enough money?"

"That and much more."

Joe hugged her. "We couldn't get pack horses, no one would lend them without a guarantee they would get them back. I bought a couple of llamas."

"I know nothing about llamas."

"You know nothing about horses."

"That's changed."

"Joe shrugged his shoulders. Treat them like a horse."

It was too late in the day to go back. Sarah stayed with the couple. "If I tell you the truth about what happened, please do not call 911 and put me in the looney bin." They reacted the same as John.

"At least I had my iPhone to show him proof."

"Who is he going to call?"

"He liked the music.

Sarah stood under the hot water until it ran out. Jane's fancy hair treatments and soaps were luxurious. As she slipped under the cool covers, her eye caught a box on the dresser. Mia's urn! In her desperation she hadn't given Mia a thought. But here was Mia, wrapping Sarah in her love. Sarah pulled the pillow and covers off of the bed and curled up and slept with Mia.

Sarah, in her new modern clothes and new hiking boots, met the llamas at the trailhead. "The owner said, "You taking all of this?

Hmph." He strapped the packs on the animals, explained how to balance the load, and check the straps. Sarah was anxious to get on her way, and only half listened.

A quick hug from her friend. "Will I see you again?" worried Jane.

"I know I have to go back and save the children. After that, I don't know what the future holds."

An hour later, Sarah realized what the llama owner didn't tell her. How to get the damn, mean, stubborn, God-forsaken animals up the mountain. The two llamas trekked pretty well for a mile. When the trail turned steep, they stopped. Sarah pulled the halter's rope, but the lead llama stood like a statue. She tried changing leads, but the second llamas stood immovable, too. Winding the main rope through their halter to apply more pressure on their noses proved useless. Sarah tried staying out of spitting range, but still found herself wiping goo off her shoulder. She put her back to their rear quarters, pushing them with all of her strength. Sarah didn't care what the llamas thought. This load had to go up the mountain. She cut a willow branch and whacked their flanks. In tandem, the llamas laid down. Holy Mother of God, what could she do? Packs had become dislodged, forcing Sarah to untie the lower straps. Magically, as the weight came off, the llamas stood meek and ready to travel, Sarah strapped the heavy packs to her back, becoming the third beast of burden. Saying an unkind, expletive ridden fair-well to the llama, she loaded the supplies carefully so the canoe wouldn't tip. She paddled unsteadily to the shore. There sat John through the shimmering light. She crossed

165

through, and he was startled, being immersed in the smartphone. A low campfire burned and Chester looked for browse.

"You are back!" John embraced her tightly. "I know you are from the future because of this." John shook the iPhone. I listened to the music. I pushed a lot of buttons that won't work. " When we are done, you have to help me with this." Sarah looked at the screen. "I can't get passed Level Three in Angry Birds."

"You taught yourself how to play Angry Birds."

"Just because I am over one hundred years younger than you, doesn't mean I can't learn your games." John backed away from her a bit. "Maybe you should have brought some nice smelling soaps from the future."

"Llamas. If you buy one stinking llama for your homestead, I will never step on your ranch again. We have to pack these supplies in a hurry. John made quick work, packing the horses with expertise. They reached Jordan in record time.

Sarah formulated a plan from the General Store. Mack said, "We have a lot of sick kids, where did ya go? We needed ya."

"I left to get the medicines. They will work to cure most of the children. Could we clear out the back room to establish a clinic? Parents can bring their children, so I can administer the different shots. Will the men ride to pass the word?"

"Sure, anything for the children."

"Get one man to bring Maddy here."

"You got it."

Jane had marked the immunization and antitoxin in big red letters. The antitoxin was for children who had active cases of diphtheria. The other was the inoculation that would prevent other children from getting it. There was no guarantee the medicines would work quickly. Sarah hoped for an 80% success rate. "John please go to Saratoga to let Dr. Hancock know what we are doing. He might not believe in the medicine. I know the lawyer in you can convince him. She looked into his hazel eyes. "Don't tell anybody." He met her gaze with a nod.

A line of families queued to see Sarah. She treated the acute cases first. Most children would benefit. Some would not survive. She gave no false hope to these families. She gently spent time telling these parents how to ease their dying child's way. Sarah dispensed hope by giving the vaccine to their remaining children with the promise of immunity from the deadly disease. Sarah instructed Maddy on administering the medicines. Her helper escorted her to the carriage, and they sped away.

John came back. "Dr. Hancock was skeptical of these medications since he never heard of them and didn't know where they came from. I could see his point, knowing what I know. I convinced him that he didn't have to recommend it, but at least notify families about the clinic." The mothers didn't need a recommendation. They flocked to the one place that would save their babies.

Sarah worked for the better part of three days. Mrs. Sullivan brought food and tea to the makeshift clinic to ensure Sarah could keep up her strength. Mack watched for lulls in the line so Sarah could take cat naps. Mrs. Colby's church committee made sure everybody in line had plenty of food, water, and prayer. John and the men rode their horses into the ground, transporting children from Saratoga. As the last of the epidemic died out, John held an exhausted Sarah in his saddle and walked Chester back to the boarding house. He settled her on her bed. Mrs. Sullivan shooed him away, stripping Sarah from her strange garb, bathed her, and dressed her in a fresh nightgown.

"You can stay in my house as long as you want, honey."

"Thank you," Sarah whispered before falling asleep for the better part of two days.

Sarah awoke rested. She headed to the Wells Fargo bank. Asking for some letterhead, she scribbled, "Dear Jane, ..." She finished the letter, put it into an envelope, and headed to the bank manager. "I need to be absolutely sure that this letter is mailed to this address in 2022."

"Miss, you must be crazy."

"I might be, but how can I ensure that this will be done?"

The bank manager finally recognized Sarah. " Aren't you the woman who brought the medicine to town? My grandson was one of the children saved," his voice quivered. Medications that no one had ever heard of? That saved our town's children? Somehow, I think this letter has something to do with that miracle. I will do everything I can to set up a system so the letter is mailed next century."

After the bank, Sarah trotted down to Mack's. She asked Mack about renting his back room for a clinic. He waved his hand. "Anybody who can save the kids of Jordan can have my back room."

"Thank you. Do you know anybody who could build me some cabinets?

Mack looked at her with a chuckle. "The best cabinet maker in town is right under your nose -John. I gotta ask you something. I looked everywhere in my catalogs. There ain't any medicines like you used. Where didja get them? I'll order more."

"There isn't anymore."

"Where did they come from then?"

Sarah hesitated. "A miracle happened this week. Though I was part of it, I don't understand how it happened. We should all just be grateful."

"Praise God."

And let the llamas go straight to hell.

She still held a grudge. Sarah knew Mack would spread the story in nothing flat, sparing her need to repeat the tale.

John rode into town to sell a horse but really see Sarah. She spied him while she was losing another checker game. "Glad to see you awake, there is work to be done," he kidded.

"Yes, there is work to be done. Can I ask yet another favor?"

"Only if it involves a chance for a kiss."

"That's a deal. I'll work hard to keep up my end of the bargain."

They entered Mack's back room and began sorting supplies. Antibiotics comprised most of the inventory. Plenty for pneumonia and dysentery. Also, drugs curing the prostitute's chief ailment of sexually transmitted disease. A few medications for laboring mothers. Rehydration kits for children with severe diarrhea. Acetaminophen for everyday use. Sarah did not pack medications for tuberculosis patients. That required pills every day for the lifetime of the person and could not be accommodated. Sarah uncovered one non-medical package – a bag of condoms. Funny, it wasn't on her list. It must have been Jane's doing. A smart choice.

"John, I have something special for us."

"What's that love?"
"You might want to have a look. This is a condom; it will prevent pregnancy."

"It's not like one of those rubber things. That's like taking a shower in a raincoat."

"It's the same principle but upgraded." He pulled the package open, feeling the thinness and flexibility.

"What's the teat on the end?"

"That's to give room for the, you know," she said suddenly shy.

"Oh, I get it,"

"I would like to use them; I don't want to get pregnant."

"Let's try them, then." He peered into the bag. "Is that all you have?"

"Yep."

"That's not near enough for as many times I intend to ravish you," he leered. "Are they going to fit.?"

She pretended to read the package. "Hmmm, extra small, I think they will do."
John tickled her ribs until she laughed, "No mas, no mas!"

As they started putting the supplies away, John reacted curiously to the packaging. When Sarah tore off the first large wrapper, he came close. "Is that plastic?"

"I guess it is. A thin plastic."

"You tore it open?"

"Sure why?"

"We do not have plastic in 1882. Who knows what we can do with it? Let me cut it open." John painstakingly cut each package with his pocketknife, so that the largest pieces could be salvaged.

Eventually, everything was unpacked, but Sarah looked into the boxes again. "Where is it? Please don't tell me they forgot it."
"What?"

"A blood pressure cuff. It is a vital medical instrument that hasn't been invented yet. She searched the boxes, but it was not there. Somehow it got missed. Sarah assessed the supplies she did have.

"How long will these medications last?"

"If we are careful they may last until winter."

"Then what?"

"I don't know. It will be hard to go back to the old ways. Children and mothers, and babies dying of curable diseases.”

"Can you get more?"

" I don't think the archway will work that way. This is it."

"Are you going to be able to stay here when all the modern medicine is gone?"

" I don't know," she said honestly. "I don't know what you are thinking either. Loving a woman 135 years older than you.

"I'll admit I have been giving it a lot of thought."

"I'd question your judgment if you didn't."

"Do you remember the first thing you told me about the future? About how people are the same now as they are in the future? That is what I think. You are the same person no matter where you are in time. You are kind, funny, and loving. You are brave."

" Me brave? I am a coward."

" Look at what you did to save the children."

"Anybody would have done that."

"Anybody didn't – you did that. There is no denying we had an instant attraction. I felt it the minute you teased me about my Scottish brogue."

I knew it when you first kissed me. I don't believe in love at first sight, but I didn't believe in time travel either."

"So," John went on, "It doesn't matter where you came from, because you are just you. I have another bigger concern. My life stays the same. I live in a time where I am used to the houses, bathrooms, stoves, rules, and prejudices. Everything that makes up a society in 1882. Everything is different for you.

Everything. How can a woman, hell, any person get used to the change."

"I don't have all of the answers right now, I know I love you and I know I want to try." They joined hands and pulled each other into a close embrace. She changed the subject. "If I give you a kiss, can I ask you for another favor?" John cocked an eyebrow. "I need cabinets built for the supplies. Nothing fancy, just something to keep them dry and in order."

"Let me see this kiss before I decide." Sarah stood a bit on her toes to reach for his mouth. She parted her lips and touched them to his. She pressed in further, and John grabbed her waist, pulling her close. The kiss was long and tender at first, but urgent at the end. They stopped when Mack politely gave an *ahem*. "John, your horse trader is here."

"Do I get my cabinets?" asked Sarah breathlessly.

"I'll build you a house for that kiss."

John held true to his word and officially courted Sarah. He bought a light buggy. Sarah thought the carriage cute but rather missed Clover.

He asked Mrs. Sullivan if she would consider being their chaperone. He would like to take Sarah to the homestead, and it would be his pleasure to show her around, too. Mrs. Sullivan perked up at the opportunity to spy on John's property. "I would be honored."

174

John, Sarah and Mrs. Sullivan, wearing a rather large straw hat, trotted to John's home. John kept up a patter of light-hearted remarks, mainly intended to charm their chaperone. Sarah was just as eager to see his cabin. An iron gate arched over the entrance. Forged metal formed the words, McIntyre and Son.

"Faither made the gate when I was a boy. His spirit looks over me every time I pass under it."

The drive was lined with quaking aspen. The green leaves shivered. John helped both ladies out of the carriage and began his tour. "Faither built the cabin mostly on his own. He started when Mother was alive; they hoped to fill it with children. The group stepped inside. The two-room cabin was meticulously constructed. The logs were evenly chinked. The wood floor lay even and smooth. An old iron stove stood by one wall. Immaculately crafted Shaker style furniture populated the room.

"Who made the furniture," Sarah breathed.

"Winters can be lonely. I needed something to do." She now knew what Mack meant about John being a cabinet-maker. "I've bought a few things, but it is a man's cabin."

"Just waiting for the right woman," suggested Mrs. Sullivan. John and Sarah tried not to look at each other.

"I have a fresh jar of lemonade cooling in the creek. It's such a warm day. Shall we sit on the porch to drink it?"

"That would be lovely." They sat on the porch for a short time. Soon Mrs. Sullivan closed her eyes and her head nodded.

"I think that is our sign."

"You didn't drug her, did you?"

"No, I took advantage of a warm day on an old lady."

They climbed bareback on Chestnut and John showed Sarah the splendors of his home. His pride of the land burst from his chest as he pointed out a rushing stream exiting from a clear spring. Acres of green hay ruffled in the hot breeze. John's dappled horses with flaxen manes fed on the verdant grass. They looked up and stomped as Chester trotted by. They rode to the top of a rolling hill. Sarah gasped at the sudden view of a snow topped mountain.

"I have ridden every inch of this place. This spot is my favorite," said John.

"If there ever was a placed blessed by God, this would be it.

"I am sure you have much grander places than this in your century."

"If I remember correctly, this land has a private gated driveway owned by some rich folk, hoarding it to themselves. It has a monstrosity of a house, 8 – 10 bedrooms, none of which are used."

"Does the gate say 'McIntyre?"

"No, just some made up ranch name."

John looked solemn and determined. "We will have to see how we can use this time travel to keep this as McIntyre land."

They circled back to the cabin, settling under a tree. Mrs. Sullivan woke; they waived at her as if they had been there the whole time.

"I saw a terrible thing when I went on rounds with Dr. Hancock the first time. Mr. Preston had beat his wife within an inch of her life."

John shook his head, "That is a terrible situation."

"Is that how our marriage would be? I would be under the authority of you?"

"That is what the law says, but it is most definitely not how it would be. Most do not hold it as true, and treat our wives as equals, or really, our betters."

"I could see a situation where my mouth could get me in trouble and make you furious. If you ever laid a hand on me, I would leave you forever."

"I would never raise a hand to you Sarah. I can't believe you would say that."

"I am afraid of living here with no legal rights."

"Tell me more." Sarah knew he was talking about the future. "I didn't just play Angry Birds. I saw many pictures I didn't understand. One picture kept popping up in the music. It looked like a man in a white suit with a circle for his head. He was holding an American flag. No matter how I looked at it, it seemed he was standing on the moon.

MTV

"That is, perhaps, man's greatest journey. Yes we have gone to the moon,"

"That is hard to believe."

"Let me take you through the story. Now you have steam engines. Trains are much more powerful now and have diesel engines.

"How does that work?"

"I have no idea. Most people don't know how anything works, they just use them. Like the smartphone Like Angry Birds and the music.

The first huge change was the automobile. It was called a horseless carriage. It had a small motor and you could sit in it and drive. Petroleum fueled it, and you didn't need horses."

"How did it work?"

"I don't know. Everybody used cars; many people had two or three. You pushed a pedal to go fast, and another one to slow down, and the wheel turned you right or left. The cars could go so fast, that one hour in a day would be three days in a horse-drawn cart." Sarah sketched several pictures of a car in the dirt. John studied them carefully. Now starts our trip to the moon. Two men, Orville and Wright built the first airplane. For the first time in history, man flew.

"Flight," John whispered.

"Yes, it was only 20 years from now. That flight only lasted 12 seconds but it was the beginning of a breakthrough journey. Airplanes were used for everything like dusting crops and transportation. They were used in war, fitted with bombs. Women built massive planes in the 1940's. Some planes weight 75,000 pounds.

John looked skeptical. "First, *Miss I Don't Know,* how are you so well versed in these details? Second, how can something that heavy fly in the air?"

"It is something that interests me, especially landing on the moon. Planes fly using the law of aerodynamics." She sketched him a picture to demonstrate the principles of airlift.

"I see how light birds use airlift, but not something that weighs 75,000 pounds."

"It has to do with the amount of engine power. Now we get into the interesting stuff."

"My head is already swimming."

"In the 1950's, Russia a made a tiny box thing called Sputnik. They figured out how to use a rocket to shoot it into space above the atmosphere."

"What is a rocket?"

"It is an engine that explodes in a controlled way located on the bottom of the missile." She drew another picture. "After that came the "Space Race." America and Russia tried to build bigger rockets, which could go further and do more things. Russia even flew a dog and a monkey into space, before they put a man in capsule." But the US quickly followed, and a man named Alan Shepard rocketed into space. Did you know you are weightless is space? You float around in the air unless you are belted to the seat." Sarah imitated an astronaut floating in space. John laughed at her, clearly not believing this tidbit. "We kept experimenting, putting a man in space in orbit all the way around the earth, next two men in space, a man walking in space, and on and on.

"Where you looking for something in space – like gold?"

"It was a true pioneering spirit. Finally a great president of the United States challenged America to put a man on the moon. In 1969, astronauts, wearing space suits like in the picture, walked on the moon. Neil Armstrong was the first man to step on the moon. As he stepped down he said, *One small step for man, one giant leap for mankind.* The words always give me goosebumps." She showed John her arm. "I have touched an actual rock brought back from the moon."

"I think you are trying to tell me the truth, But maybe you have some parts mixed up. Like floating in space. But you have changed the way I will look at the moon for the rest of my life."

"If I could connect the smart phone, I could show you a video of the men on the moon."

"Video?"

"I can show you that. Sarah looked at the battery. It read 12%. "We can still see the pictures and videos, but no more Angry Birds. The phone is almost out of juice."

"What kind of juice?"

"I mean the power is almost gone, and the phone won't work anymore."

"That's disappointing."

"Let me show you." She scrolled to the photo section, teaching John how to view the pictures and the videos.

He slowly flipped through the pictures. Most were of Mia. "Maybe you should look at these some other time," he said, sensitive to her grief. Sarah. Bracing herself, moved to view the screen. Mia smiled, laughed, and clowned it up picture by picture. John could not get over the videos, wanting to watch them continuously. "There you are, Sarah! What is behind you?"

"It is a motorcycle, like a car with two wheels."

181

The last pictures showed Mia in the hospital. Happy at first. Sleeping in bed. Pictures of her hair falling out. Finally bald.

"Did you have to cut her hair for her blood disease?"

"No, the medicine was so strong, it made her hair fall out."

"I can feel your grief. Mia was surely an angel living on earth. The pictures suddenly stopped. "What happens to the pictures when the juice is gone?"

"They stay on the phone until it gets charged again."

"How long will the phone last?"

"I have no idea. I guess quite a while if it is protected."

"Can you take a picture of me?"

Sarah smiled, "Not only can I take a picture of you, but we can do selfies. It would be a picture of us together. They laughed as they used the last of the battery to take pictures, some funny, some romantic.

"As the battery died, John asked, "Could we have taken some naughty pictures?"

"Yes, but do you want somebody to to find them in 100 years?"

"I guess not, but I would have loved to see them, even once.

John courted Sarah twice a week. Mrs. Sullivan chaperoned the longer visits, but they were free to ride on the shorter evening dates. Everybody was satisfied with the arrangement. Mrs. Sullivan protected Sarah's honor. The couple secretly looked forward to Sunday's Shaker church services.

Initially dressed in their best, they changed clothes and rode the horses up the mountains. John showed Sarah extraordinary sites. "Look at this rock" he said. "The Indians painted pictures on it thousands of years ago. Sarah examined the untouched petroglyphs with wonder. They rode to a draw where John pointed out a herd of 75 elk. I will hunt them this fall with the men for winter meat. They found Sarah's strawberry, then sweet huckleberries. John took advantage by kissing and licking the juice off her mouth. They moved no further, making love right by the blueberry bushes.

One day, they left for church on a rainy morning. Mrs. Sullivan protested, "Why would you go to church when you will get soaking wet?

"We have dry clothes at the church." Sarah wondered where the dry church would be on this chilly day. John led them to his cabin. "Ye dinnae think my home is a gud church." he grinned.

"It is an excellent place to worship, I am sure."

"I feel reluctant to come here," admitted John. "I pictured our first time at the cabin would be on our wedding night. I would pick you up in my arms and carry you to our wedding bed."

Sarah thought this was the most romantic thing ever said this, or the next century. "We can practice."

John swept her into his strong arms, "Uffdah! If I knew you were so heavy, I would have practiced earlier."

Sarah prepared a retort. John laid her on the bed, fixing his hazel eyes on their lips. He knelt above her, his powerful forearms close around her head. "I love you, Sarah May. You are everything I imagined a woman could be."

"I love you, John McIntyre. I didn't know I would have to go back to another century to find a man like you." He dipped down, imparting the sweetest kiss yet. Afterwards they lay tangled in each other's limbs.

"You are my love," he said simply. Please take my name," Sarah.

Sarah said, just as simply, "Yes."

John reached into his bedstead. "Would you wear his ring as a sign of our betrothal?" He handed her a ring with an intense gold gem. It was simply set in gold. "It is an imperial Brazilian topaz. It matches the gold in your eyes."

"Where did you get such a ring?"

I haven't seen a Zale's Jewelers here.

184

"I am a good horse trader."

"You must have traded a whole herd to get this ring."

"Will you wear it" She smiled, as he slipped it on her finger.

"When?"

"When what?" Sarah was still dazzled by the ring."

"When can we marry?"

"How about a Christmas wedding?"

"I cannae wait that long. I want you in bed with me so I can warm my feet when I come in from feeding the horses." Sarah laughed. " You winnea be laughin' this winter." The quilts kept them cozy while the lovers listened to the rain on the roof.

"We can set the date after one thing. I didn't have a proper wedding dress with my first marriage. Maybe it is silly, but I want to look like a real bride when I marry you. I can order fabric from Mack's for Mrs. Sullivan and me to sew."

"Agreed."

John whispered his fear so low, that Sarah could hardly hear it. "Please Sarah, stay, don't go."

Stretching he arm, she admired the ring. "If I go, do I have to give back the ring?"

"Yes." He grabbed at the ring. She was too quick, and held it to her heart.

"I guess I have to stay then."

The time came to conduct rounds at the brothel again. Miss Ellie was thrilled at the effect of the new drugs. The house's reputation soared. The young girl's energy livened the halls. "Dr. Sarah, your medication changed everything!"

Sarah took Miss Ellie aside. "Don't forget the medicine won't prevent pregnancy. Tell the girls they should use the diaphragm or condoms I gave you."

"I haven't had any girls pregnant for at least a month."

That didn't sound reassuring.

"Remember I told you that the medicine won't last forever."

"I remember, I remember."

"I will only have enough until winter." Winter was a long time away for a madam raking in the dough now. Sarah mounted the stairways running smack into one of the girls. They both looked up. "Adele! What are you doing here?"

"Dr. Sarah! I hope I seed you some time."

"Are you working here?"

"Yes, but not like you think. Miss Ellie gave me a real job. I help in the kitchen, do the laundry, and clean the rooms."

Sarah sighed with relief. "Do you make enough money?"

Adele looked down. "I am a little behind in room and board." She looked hopeful. "Miss Ellie is giving me a chance to catch up with the extra work."

Sara knew where this path was heading. What other job could Adele do? Not many families in town could afford a girl full-time. Maybe there were two families willing to share Adele's services. "Adele, promise me something. I may have a job for you away from the brothel."

"Really?"

"Promise me you won't be a working girl until I can talk to some women. Promise?" Adele agreed.

As the morning ended, Sarah dreaded reaching the last bedroom – Kat's. She knocked.

"Come in." Kat seemed happy enough. "Dr. Sarah, I forgot this was your day. Sarah felt cognitive dissonance between Kat's sweet voice and her past intentions. During the exam, Kat chatted away about the boom in business, the other girls, and funny stories about the clientele. After Sarah proclaimed a clean bill of health, Kat sat on the edge of the bed. She exclaimed after seeing Sarah's ring. "Oh, that is beautiful. I bet you got that from John." Sarah smiled, still distrusting Kat.

"I was married once."

Sarah tried not to look surprised. "Where is your husband now?"

"I don't know; I divorced him." Sarah knew that divorce was not that common, but not unheard of either. "Do you want to know why I divorced him?" Sarah's curiosity got the better of her.

"We lived on a farm. I worked myself to the bone tryin' to get all the work done. Why mules are treated better than farm women."

"Couldn't you get any help?"

"Help? Who could afford help? Besides, all the woman-folk worked that way."

"What did you have to do?"

"I'd get up before light and start the stove. I usually had chopped the kindlin' the night before. If I didn't, I had to split it in the dark. Then I had to start the fire, so it was warm, and to cook breakfast.

"How do you cook on one of the stoves, it seems hard?"

"You gotta watch iffen it's too hot or too cold. Bread is really tricky. I sure burned my share of loaves. Then I gotta get some water. It is ¼ mile down the road. Good water, too. I got two buckets. At first my arms were real tired, but I got strong.

"My husband came in from the barn – he got up even earlier than me. He always wanted a big breakfast and coffee. He always liked my coffee. I packed a bucket for him to take for lunch. When the haying crew came, I had to cook dinner for a dozen men!"

"Chickens needed letting out of the coop and fed. Oh, and of course I collected their eggs. Iffen I was making chicken that night, I would pick up the hen by the neck, give it a twist and break her neck." Kat demonstrated the motion. "I'd pluck her later." Sarah's stomach turned. She could never break a chicken's neck, or even cut one off either.

"Monday is washing day. I hauled all the laundry to the creek, and used a washer board. My husband's clothes were filthy from work; it took a long time. I'd drape them over the bushes to dry them. Half the time a bird would fly over and crap on a shirt. I would have to wash it again."

 I hated growing the garden, it was so much work to hoe the weeds and haul water every day. One year I let it go, and we didn't have any vegetables for winter. I sure got a beatin' from my husband for that."

"I refused to churn butter. Nobody has that much time and strength. I made him buy it iffen he wanted it." Kat went on about making sure the kitchen fire stay lit, putting up preserves and vegetables, and sewing from the interminable sewing basket.

"When I had my baby boy, I jes' couldn't do it anymore."

"You have a child?"

"Yes Dr. Sarah, the sweetest little boy with blonde hair and blue eyes. My husband named him Thomas."
"Where is he?"

Tears filled her eyes. "I don't know, "she said wistfully. Then angrily, " Of course the judge gave custody to my husband. They never let the children stay with their mother."

"What happened after you divorced?"

"I tried my hand at this and that. Women can't live on what they earn. I made friends with a nice gal who was a working girl. She said come and try it. So I did. I tell you being a whore is a hell of a lot easier than being a farm wife."

"Uh- I've got to go now. It was nice getting to know you better, Kat."

"Sure, next time we can talk about your life."

The door shut. *"Let's see how long you keep that pretty little ring on your pretty little finger now, Dr. Sarah."*

So, there is a catch to *they lived happily ever after*. Sarah didn't know a farm would entail so much work. Knowing that she could not, and let's face it, would not work like a mule. How do you fit in a medical practice, too? Or a baby, or two or three? She knew a husband worked as hard as his wife. Many times, John came courting, trying to maintain a funny banter, but was clearly tired. When she asked him, he would joke about a hard-headed horse. Or distract her with a joke. The only way through the problem was to see it first-hand. When John remarked that his mare was set to foal tomorrow, Sarah jumped at the chance. It was also a way to scope out the work situation.

Sarah avoided Mrs. Sullivan by leaving early in the morning. Clover clomped onto the homestead before light. Lanterns lit the inside of the cabin. John opened the door before she even knocked. His lips sought her broad grin. "Our first good morning kiss. Come in. I am the perfect host with hot coffee ready. We can make breakfast after morning chores." John was excited to show Sarah the working end of the homestead that was his life.

"Sounds like our day is well planned."

"Almost. The mare will decide the real schedule."

"Do you think she will foal today?"

"Pretty sure. The momma is restless, sweating, and starting to produce milk."

"Don't you want to stay with her?"

"Bill will work around the barn until we have morning chores done."

191

"I hope we don't miss it. I have never seen a foaling before."

"Not much different than a baby being born, is it?"

Modern births are a bit different.

They lingered over their coffee. Sarah eyeballed the stove. "I have no idea how to use something like that. It looks intimidating."

"No denying you need to keep a close eye on it. There is a new one that will keep the water warm. Maybe we can buy one next year."

Sarah noticed the pile of kindling. "How long does it take to make dinner?"

"If you keep the stove hot all day it isn't too bad. Say I catch you a big batch of fish. You could fillet them. You would use cornmeal from the bin – he gestured towards a group of canisters. Use egg and milk with it to coat it ,and fry it with lard."

"Where do I get the eggs?"

"I am buying them from Mack's, but you could raise chickens if you want."

"How about milk?"

"Betsy is out there. Bill usually milks her. We keep the eggs and butter in the cooling shed out back."

"What else do you like to eat? Bill and I like fresh bread, but we purchase it from Mack's, too. There's nothing like coming home to the smell of freshly baked bread. Faither had a woman to help when I was a boy. She made the most incredible chocolate cake that I have ever eaten, before or since. Man, I would love a piece of that cake."

I wonder if he likes cake mix.

"So, what do you think, an hour to cook dinner?"

"I guess it would depend on how much was accomplished during the day. Of course, there are dirty dishes afterward. I don't like to wash, but I am a great dish dryer." John was so involved in telling his story about cabin life, he didn't notice a growing expression of dismay on Sarah's face.

"I made dinner quite a bit differently at home." John leaned forward, always interested in the future.

"Mia was going through this big macaroni and cheese phase. I put the already-mixed bowl in something called a microwave oven. You just turned a dial, the oven turned on, and you had a complete meal in 60 seconds. If we had fish, I would take a package out of our freezer. "A freezer was like your cold room, but it cooled food until it froze like ice."

"Is that how you stored food?"

"A lot of it. Cans and plastic, too. I could cook an entire meal in 5 minutes."

"How did it work?"

"Something called radio waves, and no, I don't know how it worked."

"All of that doesn't sound very appetizing. I like my fresh trout fried in a pan."

"On my days off, I made more elaborate meals, none that took more than forty minutes. Clean-up was another wonder. We used a machine called a dishwasher. You just put in the dishes, glasses, and pans, and they were washed and dried automatically. There were also two machines that washed and dried your clothes."

"Sure seems like life is easier in the future."

"It gave people a lot more free time. I could play with Mia, Mike tinkered on his motorcycle; we watched a lot of tv or played on the computer.

"Didn't you use your smartphone to read everything you could?"

"Though many people achieved incredible things, so many people were dumbed down by 2022. I called it an idiocracy. At the very same time I was guilty of watching insipid reality shows on tv," she said ruefully.

"What's tv?"

194

"I need a whole day to tell you about the entertainment industry."

It was past time to start morning chores. They strode to the barn in the dark. John lit a lantern, hanging it outside the door. Sarah noticed a bandage wrapped around John's knuckles. "What did you do to your hand?"

"Let's just say some of us persuaded Mr. Preston to leave his wife alone." Sarah shivered at the thought of vigilante justice.

Sarah watched as John worked each stall, placing oats in the bin. There seemed to be a different formula for each of the eight horses. He murmured to them. They perked their ears and nuzzled his hands. John motioned Sarah to the last stall. There stood the pregnant mare. She was nipping at her flanks and had a sheen of sweat on her neck. Sarah could see her teats were swollen.

"How's our girl this morning?" asked John.

"I reckon today is the day." Sarah felt excited at the prospect.

"Bill, if you finish out here, Sarah and I will start breakfast."

"Sounds good. I'll do a good job in exchange for a hearty breakfast." Back in the house, John explained how he was preparing food. He put Sarah in charge of the bacon. Despite Sarah's intent concentration, she managed to burn it.

"I'm so sorry, I really tried."

"No sense crying over spilt milk or burnt bacon. But you are going to have to explain that one to Bacon Bill."

Bill politely didn't mention the bacon at breakfast. The dishes were washed using the last of yesterday's water. True to claim, John was an excellent dryer. Sarah muttered about running hot and cold water. The sun rose as they walked to the barn. John haltered Chestnut, telling Sarah to do the same for Clover. They walked the horses to the pasture. The warm summer morning made Sarah picture herself taking on the duty. "Do you keep the horses in the barn in the winter?"

"Nope, unless the weather is very bitter, we take them out. Winter is harder because we have to haul hay to the pastures." That job didn't seem as pastoral as Sarah initially thought. I am fortunate that I have a full-time creek that runs through the property. No hauling water for livestock. In the winter, I chop an access hole. That creek is a time saver."

"When we put the garden in, we will have to haul more water for the vegetables, though." Sarah remained silent. Kat had not exaggerated her life. They reached the pasture, letting the horses go free. Chestnut trotted around, kicking her heels. Clover walked over to the nearest grass and started to graze.

"What about water for the house?"

"The spring runs a bit further up the road. "Two buckets usually gets us through the day. Maybe more if we want a bath." John leered, "Now I haven't thought about bath nights."

Sarah laughed, picturing them both fitting in one of those tubs. "Do you have bubble bath?"

"That sounds intriguing."

The single draft horse was pastured last. A piercing whistle came from the barn. "Rodeo time!" called Bill. The mare laid on an extra thick bed of straw.

"Is it time?" asked a breathless Sarah.

"It's like a baby, you know it's coming, just not exactly when."

"I didn't realize until I saw all of your horses that they were the same breed."

"They are called Appaloosa horses. They are bred by the Nez Pierce Indians. They are much prized by the tribe and are rarely sold or traded. The most valuable ones have black and white spots and flaxen manes and tales. I never knew what Faither traded to get his herd started. But slowly he built his herd. The horses are considered valuable, and when we think we can sell one, there are many buyers. They are very even-tempered when they are trained, adding more to the value. We make a steady living at it. Bill is quite the horse-whisperer."

"I thought you were a horse whisperer," said Sarah.

"Bill taught me everything I know."

"Don't you forget it boy," Bill intoned.

"Their manes and tails are incredible."

"Ach they look beautiful, but they come with a lot of work. We spend a lot of time grooming them. Now that you are here we may be able to bring two more horses on board."

Before Sarah had time to respond about her doubts, Bill calmly said, "It's started." Sarah watched as little feet pushed rhythmically through the mare's vulva. As the process continued, she saw a nose. John and Bill were patient. John whispered, " We think the best thing to do is to let nature take its course. We only intervene when there is trouble."

In no time at all, the foal lay on the ground, Momma licking the caul. Bill remarked, "She isn't getting up." They watched intently, soon seeing signs of continued labor. Another set of hooves began emerging.

"Damn John, you told me she didn't have twins."

"Nope, the mare surprised me."

The horse licked the caul off the second foal, as the first tried out its legs. Sarah laughed at the comical efforts and determination despite frequent falls. So, the mare stood with her two offspring suckling their first meal greedily. The three humans and three animals basked in the magic of the moment.

Bill broke the spell. "I've got to harness Minnie to pull that stump."

John nodded. I have a whole day's work to do; we lost a lot of time with the foaling. Sarah, I know it is new to you, but do you think you could fix a simple dinner? There are cans of meat and jars of vegetables, bread, and things like that. I haven't gotten the water for the day, would you mind hauling that?"

All right, how hard could this be? Forget the burnt bacon. I'll get the water first. Sarah found two buckets and strode purposefully to the spring. The water was plentiful and cold. She took a long drink before filling the buckets. *Better than Dasani any old day.* She headed home, a bucket in each hand. It didn't take long until the wire handles bit into her fingers. Resettling the bucket on less tender areas didn't help; soon her hands were blistered from the handles. Her arms began to ache from the weight of the buckets. Positioning her shoulders in different positions didn't improve the situation either. Sarah had to rest every 25 steps or so. This was even worse than Kat said.

Nearing the cabin, she decided to make a long dash. Her foot caught on her long skirt, causing her to tumble to the ground. One bucket tipped over completely, the other sloshed to half full. "Shit, shit, shit!" Sarah thought of Kat's description of hauling water but thought reality was much worse. Dinner required water, but Sarah could not haul two more pails. She compromised by toting ¾ of a bucket back, wincing all the way.

Now the stove needed heating, but how hot? How do you regulate the temperature? The ordered pantry boasted jars with neatly printed labels. She noted pieces of plastic used to hold objects to the wall. She chose canned beef, green beans, and corn. A loaf of bread lay under a towel sacking. Removing the cloth, she saw bits of mold clinging to the crust. At home, this would be tossed. *I can't imagine the waste of bread.* Sarah cut away the mold. The bread now resembled Swiss cheese. If she used enough butter from the cooling house, maybe they won't notice the holes.

Time to open the can. The can opener lay in the drawer. Sarah studied it. How in the hell did this thing work? She supposed you punched the tin with the sharp end. But what then? Clutching the can to puncture it, the can caromed to the floor. Next time she held it between her knees. With a mighty effort, she stabbed the can. The opener skittered off the tin and stuck into her hand. Blood flowed down her wrist. Jesus Christ!

Sarah reached for the cloth that covered the bread to staunch the flow of blood. Holding her hand high, she searched the cabin for a cloth to wrap around the wound. Didn't heroines tear their petticoats for a bandage? When the bleeding slowed, she took a knife and tried to cut an even strip. The throbbing in her hand only allowed her to tear a strip that led all the way to her thigh. Kat didn't tell me about lethal kitchen instruments.

OK, no meat. The damn men could have vegetables and bread, and the leftover burned bacon if they wanted it. She picked up the green beans to open the jar. The lid stuck tightly. Hampered by her hand, she couldn't unscrew the lid. The jar slipped and shattered on the floor at her last attempt.

In all the confusion, Sarah forgot the stove. First, it was a burnt smell, then she was horrified to see smoke pouring out. She ran to the pantry for flour to pour over the flames. The smoke began to build. It did not take John five minutes to smell the smoke from the barn. He sprinted to the cabin, looked at the stove, and opened the damper. His heartbeat visibly in a vein in his temple. "What the hell," he trailed off looking at the destruction of his cabin and Sarah. Flour covered the stove and most of the floor leading to the pantry. Smoke choked the air. Sarah's torn dress exposed one leg. His mother's precious tea towel was drenched in blood. Glass and green beans covered the floor.

"What happened?"

"I fixed your dinner, can't you see, "Sarah retorted, smoke burning her eyes.

"You nearly destroyed my house," John aimed to be even-tempered.

"I cannot, in any way shape, or form, believe that you want your wife to work like this. "Look at the blisters on my hands from the buckets." She thrust them under his face."

"Why didn't you use the gloves?" He pointed to leather gloves hanging by the door.

"What difference would it make when the water is so heavy the draft horse couldn't carry it.?"

"You almost burned the cabin to the ground. God knows how long it will take to get the smell of smoke out of here."

"I am supposed to know how to use this stove by ESP?"

"What the hell is ESP? How did you cut your hand?"

"Another ancient mechanism I don't know how to use. I spliced my hand to pieces with that can opener."

"I see you bled onto one of the few pieces of linen I have let from my mother."

That gave Sarah pause, but her temper overcame her guilt. "I tried to find another bandage, but all I managed to do was destroy my dress."

" If you don't know how to do something, why didn't you just ask?" John's voice rose.

"You expect women to work like mules!"

"Why would I want you to work like a mule? I expect you to have better sense than," he flung his arms open, "than this!"

"I cannot work in a century-old kitchen. I can work long, and I can work hard, but I cannot function under conditions like this."

"What do you mean conditions like this? Like working in the home and land that I love since the day I was born? Everything was great when we took time off to make love with the wonders of the homestead. But for every hour of fun, there are forty hours of work."

"Forty hours! This was just three for dinner. How can I work as a doctor and pop out a couple of kids, too!"

"I expect a partner who will share the love of our home and land. A partner who will share the burden and ease the way."

"John, I don't see how I can manage."

"So you think you can't make it in this century? Do you need to go back to your dish waves and washers? Instead of greeting your husband with a kiss, will you call him on the smartphone to come home? Once the medicines are gone, are you going to give up on the children because you can't cure their sickness?"

Sarah cried out, "That isn't fair John, and you know it!"

"Isn't it?"

Self–righteous anger stood between them.

"Do you think this work is below you?" asked John, showing no emotions.

"Kat was right. It is easier being a whore than a farm wife."

John's voice turned to ice. "Then you can be a whore, or you can go back to your century." Sarah carefully removed the topaz ring and set it on the windowsill. The sun touched it, and the rays reflected the gold.

Sarah made it as far as the gate before the tears started. Small at first, but then the floodgates opened as her heart broke. How could she ever have thought that love would work in 1882? How could she let herself love a man, however enlightened, still saw women brought 19th-century eyes? How could her life be such a mess again?

Sarah left Clover at the livery and began to walk home. She was overcome with nausea. But it was different, a nausea that came from the past. One that bought her back to another time in a future century. One that brought a vision of Mia.
Sarah barely made it to her bedroom before vomiting into the basin. Nausea and heartbreak paralyzed her body. There was a tap on the door. Mrs. Sullivan asked, "Are you all right Sarah?"

"I think I have food poisoning," she croaked.

"Can I help?"

"No, I will lay here for a while."

Later that evening, her landlady tapped again. Sarah stayed quiet, as if asleep. Instead, she lay awake all night, thinking of the bitter words between her and John. She cried into her pillow, trying to muffle the sounds in a boarding house with paper-thin halls.

The queasiness returned with a vengeance when Sarah awoke. This time Mrs. Sullivan came in without knocking. "I brought some peppermint tea. It will settle your stomach." She did not express surprise at Sarah's condition. "Let me help you wash your face and tidy up. Sarah would not look into her eyes. The peppermint tea eased the nausea a bit, however, she was unable to get out of bed crippled by a broken heart and not knowing the way forward. The relationship was irreconcilable. John did not want her knowing she would never be the partner he needed. She erroneously thought that love could span 135 years. It sure sounded good in romance books, but that is what this was – a fictional book.

Her baby was anything but fictional. She did not need any instant pregnancy test to affirm this child in her womb. What should I do? *Stay or Go?* John hit a tender chord. Could she stand to see children die from preventable diseases when the medicines ran out? Was she a coward to run away when Jordan needed her here? The next thought brought tremors. How many women would die in agonizing childbirth like Beatrice? Was her own impending delivery the next? What if her child died of a common disease? She could not bear to lose another child. Sarah spent another night in mental agony, torn between each no-win situation.

On the third morning, Mrs. Sullivan arrived with tea. "John is here. He was here yesterday, too. Yesterday morning and yesterday afternoon. Do you want to see him?" Sarah shook her head, miserably. "I think this tea will help. It is Maddy's special concoctions. Sarah sipped it and the nausea immediately slipped away.

"Do you have something to tell me?" Mrs. Sullivan asked. Once again kindness was Sarah's undoing.

"The tears spilled over her red-rimmed eyes. "John and I, we - we, broke up."

"I saw your beautiful ring was gone. Is there anything else?"

"I am pregnant," she said flatly." I am so sorry to be a disappointment. You have been wonderful to me; I have betrayed your trust."

Stay or Go?

"What are you going to do? I know John loves you, surely it can be worked out."

Sarah shook her head, "It is done."

"John will marry you now that there is a baby."

"He doesn't know."

"That's the answer. He will make it right when you tell him. He is an honorable man. And think, no one can work in Jordan as an unmarried mother. You will lose all of your patients."

"Where I come from, we don't have to marry men because we are pregnant."

"Men won't marry pregnant women in Kansas?" She asked knowingly.

"I guess I don't know." Sarah bit her lip.

"Where are you really from?"

Sarah stayed silent, weighing how far she could go with this dear woman. "Mrs. Sullivan, I want to tell, but I don't know how to explain it in a way that anybody can understand."

"Does John know?"

"Yes."

"Is that what the fight was about?"

"No, he has known for quite a while."

" He loves you for who you are, no matter where you come from."

"At least he used to love me."

"I know that you came to Jordan in clothes I have never seen before. I saw you didn't understand how to manage things that every woman knows. I know there was a dangerous journey to bring back wondrous medicines that we have never seen before. You were terribly brave during the diphtheria epidemic." Sarah wondered if Mrs. Sullivan had guessed the truth. "More importantly, I saw the compassion when you cared for Mrs. Crosby. You are knowledgeable enough to take on our whole town as a doctor. Your kindness helped Adele. Even though we didn't always see eye to eye, you have always shown respect to me. You are faithful to God, going to Quaker services every Sunday. Sarah, there is a capacity for great love in your heart. These are the things that make me love you. Not the mysteries of your origin." Sarah, in her grief, lay her head on Mrs. Sullivan's lap, who said, "I feel like you are a daughter to me."

"I feel the same way."

"I had a daughter once."

Sarah lifted her head. "You did? Where is she now?"

"I buried her in the church cemetery five years ago. She died in childbirth. My grandson didn't live to the age of one."

"Dear God," said Sarah. "I don't know what to do. There are no right answers."

"Pray to God dear. He always knows."

With no God to pray to, Mrs. Sullivan's dead daughter decided Sarah's path. She packed Maddy's tea, found her modern clothes, and slipped out of the house. She would go home; her adventure would be over. There might not be a happy ending, but John's baby would be delivered in a modern hospital and receive modern medical care.

Another shadow slipped out of the house that night. A cloaked girl silhouetted by the moon made her way to Miss Ellie's. Kat greeted her at the back door. The girl whispered in Kat's ear. Money changed hands. Kat's face contorted in anger.

Sarah wended her way up the trail. Maddy's tea helped her nausea better than any modern medicine. It took more than two hours to reach Mirror Lake with her need to rest more frequently. Bread and cheese would taste good right now. Even the moldy bread at John's. I can eat gummy Wonder bread in just a little bit longer. She decided to rest at the lake. Laying on her back, the half-moon and zillions of stars populated the unpolluted night stay. With no sleep for three nights, she dozed. So many faces entered her dream. Miss Ellie, Mack, Beatrice, Mary, so many children. Even Clover trotted through. John's presence wound through the dream community. He stood by her in her time of need. Mrs. Sullivan telling her to pray. White Buffalo whispering the need to find her own path.

The decision couldn't be made without intuition and self-trust. Sarah felt selfish when she thought only of herself. The path was crowded with people she was learning to love. Now a little person depended on her decision to stay or go. What would her baby say? What would John's baby say? A child with no audible voice, but an insistent spirit whispered in her heart.

Stay, stay, stay.

John had a right to hear his child. But what if they took her baby away from her like Kat?

Stay, stay, beat the tiny heart.

Sarah stood, adjusted her pack, with her decision made. She headed down the mounting towards Jordan, and wherever her path might lead. She made it down the mountain quickly. Passing the saloon on her way back to Mrs. Sullivan's, Kat's face flashed in front of hers.

"You didn't believe my warning, did ya? You think you can keep him with a bastard child?"

"Kat, what are you talking about? Ho- how did you know?"

"I've got something on most everybody in this town. Now I have you." Sarah felt a sickening blow on her temple. Her knees buckled into unconsciousness. Kat signaled for two men waiting in a wagon. "You know where to take her. I'll be there in the morning. Be sure to use the chloroform to keep her knocked out. The men drove a few blocks when Sarah awoke. She slashed their faces and kneed one in the groin. It took a scant second for the men to subdue her with the chemical. But the men were not alone. Adele stood on the porch watching the scene, half in shadow. Kat leaned by the doorway.

"Kat! They kidnapped Dr. Sarah!"

"Why would you think that?" Kat asked lazily.

" I saw her fighting two men!"

"Are you sure it was Sarah?"

"I, I think so."

"Was she wearing a dress?"

That stopped Adele. "No, it were pants. But her hair was Dr. Sarah's!"

"Adele, if the person wore pants, it was probably some drunk cowboys fighting. Besides, I saw her walk to Mrs. Sullivan's an hour ago."

"I guess mebbe I was mistook." Adele turned away. Kat had to be right, but the hair looked just like Dr. Sarah's."

Sarah woke on a mattress that smelled of urine and excrement. Her head felt split in two, so much that her eyes couldn't focus. The sickening sweet odor about her face culminated in vomiting. She turned her head to the dirt floor to add to its filth.

"Looks like the chit is awake again," a deep voice drawled.

"Think we should use that stuff?" A higher voice asked.

"Nah, she's too sick to do anything. Screaming won't help around here."

My God, where is here? Sarah's fingers touch the goose egg lump on her temple. What was that smell? She dry heaved again. "Sir? May I have some water?" Sarah asked timidly.

The deep voice said, "I guess it won't hurt none." He tossed her a canteen.

Her hands shook as she tried to open the container. Sulfurous water poured into her mouth, causing another fit of vomiting.

"My water ain't good enough for you?"

"Here she comes," said the high-pitched man.

Kat strode into the crib, gloating at Sarah, "You didn't take my warning the first time, did ya? You took John from me, and now it is time to pay the bill."

"Kat, I didn't take John, I had no choice."

" You had the same choice I had. John was my ticket out of that hell hole. You stole that ticket."

Sarah had no answer. In a perverse sense, she was guilty as charged. She competed with Kat for the prize and benefits of snagging John McIntyre. "Now you think you have John wrapped around your finger ready to walk down the aisle as a respectable married woman. I get to stay in this snake pit selling myself to the highest bidder night after night. Sarah could not refute this truth either. You may think you are so smart, Dr. Sarah. One night in a brothel ain't even close to knowing what a real whore does. "Do you know where you are?" Sarah didn't but knew it was very bad. "We are at a crib behind the railroad station."

"No -Kat -No!"

"One night's work here will barely make up all the months of my gentleman visitors. If that doesn't kill you, we'll have a go again at the next train."

"Kat you have to stop," Sarah sobbed. "I am pregnant."

"So was I, " Kat spit out bitterly. They took my son away from me just because I was a woman. I got pregnant again, cuz I am a working girl. I took a cure that gutted me 'til I thought my insides would fall to the floor. How long do you think until I get to take that medicine again?"

"I can get you help, like Adele."

"You goin' to get all my babies back? Kat unexpectedly caught her breath in the back of her throat, fighting back dark torment. She walked into the crib, avoiding the filth. "Here is my justice. You will lie there waiting' for that train. When it comes, you'll know that twenty men will have you as fast and as hard as they can. Some will like you so much they may come back. Think you will feel the difference between a man's juice and the blood of your baby dripping down your leg?"

Sarah's mind snapped from reality, drifting above the ramshackle crib. Lights shone in the sky. Mike, then Mia. Mike's path cut off. Mia's light, strong at first, then fading from the sky, her precious Mia. A thin shaft drifted to the mountain lake shining on the heavy cold gun. The light strengthened again hovering over the brothel, mirroring her path with Kat. Many small lights appeared, touching the boarding house and the lives of her patients, and her children. No light beamed as strong as the twin hazel lights from the homestead. Her mind returned to face her torture with a path clearly chosen. She didn't know how, but she would do anything to save her child.

Adele tossed and turned in her bed. Her dreams were infused with blue jeans sprouting chestnut hair. She awoke at sunrise, sitting blear-eyed on the edge of her bed. Kat shouldn't be awake, but Adele wanted to ask one more time about the fight. Padding over to Kat's door, Adele knocked softly. After no answer, she gingerly turned the knob. The door swung wide, revealing an empty room. Adele cursed the tangles in her boots in her haste to reach the boarding house. "Mrs. Sullivan! Mrs. Sullivan!" Adele wailed. "Somethin's happened to Dr. Sarah!"

The boarding house owner rushed to the door, surprised to see Adele. "Why are you back in Jordan?"

"Please help. Somethin's happened to Dr. Sarah. We have to find her right away!" Mrs. Sullivan folded her arms over her chest. The color drained from her face as Adele spilled her tale. She ran to Sarah's room, finding a note written in Sarah's peculiar handwriting.

My dear Mrs. Sullivan,

Stay or Go?

I am going back to the place where my baby will be born safe and protected from illness. A permanent hole in my heart opens as I leave all that I have come to love. I will tell my baby everything about you and Jordan, so he or she will know what love really means.

Sarah May

Mrs. Sullivan opened the trunk at the end of the bed, rummaging to the bottom. The queer clothes were gone! Did Sarah flee? Or did something happen to her before leaving? Adele's face was covered in tears. Mrs. Sullivan took her by her shoulders, shaking them firmly." Adele, calm yourself. Who is Kat, and why do you think she would take Sarah?

"Kat is one of the girl's at Miss Ellie's. She was mad when Mr. Johnny picked Sarah instead of her."

"Picked her where?"

"At Miss Ellie's."

"Sarah was at Miss Ellie's?"

Adele nodded. "Jes' one night. Johnnie picked her, and Kat said she would get even with Dr. Sarah."

Mrs. Sullivan struggled to digest this news. Was Sarah a prostitute at a brothel? Was that her secret? Did John frequent Miss Ellie's?

"I don't think Sarah had been at a whore house before. I had to dress her and do everythin'. She didn't know how to get a man to pick ya. She must have known somethin' because Mr. Johnnie sure picked her.

"Where would Kat take Sarah?" Mrs. Sullivan knew little of the world of prostitution. "Adele, if you were Kat, where would you take her?"

Adele shivered. "I would take her to the worst place in the world. The place Dr. Sarah found me. The railroad cribs."

"What is a crib?"

"When you cain't work at a parlor house anymore, you go to the railroad. You have a shanty where you wait for the train to stop. The men come into your crib, as many as you can take. They only pay enough to get you through to the next time. You don't get to choose. It's…it's the most horrible hell anybody can imagine." Mrs. Sullivan stood frozen. Never in her life could she believe a thing like this could exist. Might Sarah be there?

"Girls! Start contacting the prayer chain as fast as God gave you feet. Tell them to go to the railroad shanties in any way possible. Tell them Sarah is in danger. Go! Go!" The girls fled to their connections on the prayer chain. It was well practiced for times of need. The entire women's congregation began their race against a train, due in half an hour.

Mrs. Sullivan ran as fast as her corseted body allowed to the General Store. "Mack, Sarah's been kidnapped down by the railroad. Hurry, send the men. Get John!" She crossed the street to the livery, tossed off the years, mounted a horse and galloped away. Following Mrs. Sullivan, women were mounted on horses of every size and ability wearing all types of bridles and

215

harnesses. Next, were those driving in wagons and buggies. Mrs. Colby led this charge, spurring her driver to greater speeds until the carriage rocked precariously over the rocks. The women's faces were set in cold determination, a sisterhood that knew no social bounds. The armada of women reached the line of cribs as the trained steamed to a stop. They created a continuous barrier between the men in the train and the women in the cribs.

Men jumped off the train but were repelled by a diplomatic *leave these women alone* which was interspersed with cruder comments about dismemberment should they touch a girl. Confusion mounted. The men soon got the idea that their prize was to be denied.

The prostitutes added to the chaos. Women decried their access to their sole means of money. Others hid deep in their shanties, fearful of the beating they would receive from their flesh peddler if they didn't hand over enough money at the end of the night. Many sat motionless, any feeling of hope or rescue long exhausted from their souls.

"Mack had directed Tommy to round up the men in the town. He headed to search for John himself. Mack spied Bill in the lower horse pasture. "Bill! Sarah has been kidnapped. She is at the crib by the train. Find John right away. It looks bad."

"You go look in the south fields Mack." Bill threw his leg over his horse, galloping bareback to where he hoped to find John.

John sat with his back to a tree, feeding a stick to a small campfire. Chestnut grazed near him. He took no joy in the presence of his horse. "I'll have to sell her," he thought miserably. "I can't stand looking at the color of her coat being the same as her hair." Even with that thought, he knew he would never part with one of the few tangible memories of Sarah. If only that smartphone worked, he could see the pictures of that happy day together. "What was that song on Music Chestnut? It was the insect group…Yesterday, that was it. That's how it feels." Chestnut swished his tail in sympathy.

John thought he knew about heartbreak. A terrible pain that slowly subsided until equilibrium was restored. Scarred on the inside, but functional again on the outside. But this - this. How could he have given her such a cruel ultimatum? Was Sarah back in 2022 already? Totally unreachable? No way to go on bended knee to beg her forgiveness. No way to beseech here to stay. He now understood her heartbreak at the loss of Mia. Sarah and Mia had so much love and life, stolen in six short weeks. Sarah left the hospital with empty arms driving home to silence. She found the courage and endurance to try again. He thought he knew her so well, yet only in understanding her loss did he see the strength of her spirit.

Showering gravel disrupted his mourning. "John! They kidnapped Sarah, you have to go!" commanded Bill.

John needed only one detail. "Where?"

"The cribs by the railroad." John jumped on Chestnut. For the first time in his life, he abused the horse for every second of speed he could wring from its body.

Stay or Go?

Mrs. Colby stood her carriage, Using the voice of her deceased pastor husband, she stilled the crowd, "Leave all you degraded fool, you are an abomination of God and are not wanted here.

"I'll abominatin' her too, iffen I want to," snicker one man.

Mrs. Colby turned on him. "Do you believe in God?"

"Sometimes, when I am not abominatin." The men laughed.

"Do you have a sister?"

He hesitated. "I have two."

"Where are they?"

"One is married in Montana."

"What is her name?"

"Elise."

"Is she pretty?" The background sounds of the men quieted. He couldn't help, but puff up with pride, telling her about his sister's dainty hands.

"What if you entered a crib and found her there?"

"Wa'll that's impossible, she's in Montana."

"Do you think any of these girls have brothers who love them, like you?" The men stepped back into the crowd, no longer willing to stand under the righteous eye of Mrs. Colby. Taking her cue, the women shamed the men into retreat. Nevertheless,

218

both sides rattle their guns. As the town's men came into view, the railroaders decided that maybe this rendezvous wouldn't hold the pleasures they hoped. They skulked away. Over half the prostitutes left their cribs to follow them.

The situation was anything but diffused at the far end of the cribs. Mrs. Sullivan forced her horse through the crowd, arriving at the last crib. "Sarah?" she called.

"Mrs. Sullivan?" croaked a weak voice.

The fierce landlady spoke from the height of her horse. "I demand you let her go."

"What makes you think we are gonna do that?" asked the low-voiced man.

There was no time for argument. Pulling her gun from her skirts, she aimed for his knee, and did not miss her target. "Does anybody else want to go through life without a knee?"

The action quelled everybody except Kat, who aimed her gun at Sarah's temple. "You can shoot out as many knees as you want. I have the real prize here."

The crowd threw themselves to the side as John roared through the cribs until he saw Sarah. He instantly assessed the situation. A man held his knee rolling in pain. Mrs. Sullivan's determined expression. Inside, Sarah lay helpless on the floor, pupils dilated with fear. And Kat pointed a gun directly at her head.

"Kat," he said softly.

Stay or Go?

She lifted her eyes and gave an involuntary moue at his presence. Why'd you pick her Johnnie?" she asked bitterly.

I think it was because we had the same color eyes," he said honestly and with respect.

She appeared less sure of herself.

"It's over now, Kat." John's smooth voice appealed. The gun wavered in her hand. "It doesn't have to end like this."

Sweat carried her makeup down one side of her face. Tears spilled over her eyelids, channeling thick dark mascara. Her mouth twisted. "You always liked me in pink, didn't you Johnnie?" she asked wistfully.

"You were always real pretty in your pink dress Kat," John responded with sincerity.

It happened so fast that John couldn't do anything to stop her. A single gunshot rang out. John fell protectively over Sarah. Sarah cried out as Kat fell, dead from her own hand. John ignored Kat's body. He clenched Sarah to his chest. "Sarah are you still with me?"

She heard his voice as it was a great distance away. "Can't breathe," she muttered. John loosened his hold long enough to look at her for injuries. He lifted her onto Chestnut, still lathered and heaving, and made their way home.

John gently placed Sarah on the bed. Bill began heating water. John stripped off her filthy clothes. He bathed Sarah as carefully as the mare cleaned her new foals. In her reverie, Sarah felt the drizzle of warm water and smelled the strong soap. *"No pretty soaps where llamas come from,"* her mind wandered in confusion. He washed her hair, combing the chestnut strands back with his fingers. He dressed her in one of his shirts. Tucking the quilt around her, he sat next to the bed in the rocking chair Faither had made for his mother. Holding his head in his hands, he waited for her to wake, waiting for her decision, did she still want to go?

Sarah half opened her eyes. It seemed to be the middle of the night. There was John, silhouetted against the lamplight. How could she have wronged a man such as this? "John?" she whispered."

He started, then looked her over anxiously, "Are you all right?"

"I think I am."

"Let me get you some broth." He helped Sarah settle into an upright position as she took a few sips.

"Mrs. Sullivan's?" raising her eyebrows.

"Of course, who else?" They chuckled.

Sarah shivered despite the warm soup. "Let me get you another quilt."

"You keep me warm."

He slid into bed. Sarah felt comforted by his familiar heat. He held her for a long while, their touch a healing balm to their battered love.

Stay or Go?

They turned to face each other. Words flew together at once. "I'm so sorry", "your clothes were ruined." They tried again. "If you want to go back,", "All I really wanted."

"You go first," said John.

"No, this time I really need you to go first."

John looked at her quizzically but started. "Your modern clothes were ruined; we have to burn them. When you go back again, maybe Mrs. Sullivan can make something that will work." Sarah could see the pain in his hazel eyes as he spoke about her leaving. She acknowledged the magnanimity of his heart to respect her wishes.

"John, I am sorry from the depth of my heart. I made a terrible decision about leaving. I was frightened about living alone and about staying in this century. Fear ruled my head. I wish I could apologize to Kat, too."

"You don't blame yourself for Kat, do you?"

"Partly. I took her hope for a chance to escape, and she was trapped. I suffered like that when Mia died."

"Did you go to the lake?"

"Halfway. I stopped at Mirror Lake to rest. I lay there and thought of everybody I have met in Jordan. I even thought of Clover! But mostly I thought of you. I listened deep inside, and I found a quiet answer."

John looked at her with anxiety.

Stay or Go?

"There was a tiny voice saying, stay, stay, stay. It was the voice of our child."

John's face lit in ecstatic astonishment. "You mean you are pregnant? It is a baby; it is our baby!" John didn't exactly make sense in his joy. Sarah saw his happiness and his immediate love for their child. It was at that moment, she knew her baby was right. She would stay.

"Sarah!" He kissed her deeply, then stopped short.

"Do you still want to go back?" Before Sarah could shake her head, he plowed on. "I understand why you would go. It would be safer and you wouldn't die like Mother; our baby could learn to go to the moon, and do so much more. John looked fierce. "When you go back I will discover a way to go with you. I will make White Buffalo tell me how to go to 2022. I will find you and our baby and live life your way. I will take care of you, and make a living. make a living – playing Angry Birds!" They both laughed at the absurd notion that had popped out of his mouth.

"I see things differently now," said Sarah softly. "I remember this handsome man outside a Quaker church on a beautiful pond. He kept saying nonsense things like Sarah fair. He had a great idea for us. Is that offer still open?"

John locked his eyes on hers.

John loves a woman oh so rare,

Her smile, freckled face, and chestnut hair.

223

Stay or Go?

Her hazel eyes,

Like mine, surprise,

Will you wed me Sarah fair?

"Yes, Yes!"

Sarah asked everybody she could find. No one knew Kat's given name. Sarah's heart was saddened that no one knew the real Kat. She would be buried anonymously. A churchyard burial would have been forbidden, but Sarah's rescue opened the eyes of the town of Jordan.

When Sarah asked for permission, Mrs. Sullivan invited her to a church committee meeting.

"Sarah, though the circumstances were difficult, the committee wants to thank you."

"Thank me? For putting everybody in danger?" asked Sarah incredulously.

"No dear, for opening our eyes to the true need in our town. All these years we have patted ourselves on our back for shipping Bibles to unknown Africans or supporting missionaries to heathen Indians – no offense to your father. We didn't see the real need right under our nose." Mrs. Sullivan continued, "We have been working to save the women in the brothel and the cribs. Not to save them from going to hell, but to aid their lives. About 2/3 of the women left the railroad camp, presumably to set up another crib. That is sad; we will pray for them. We found about 1/4 of the women had advanced stages of tuberculosis. We are sending them to sanitariums in the north to regain their health. Or at least to have a place to die in dignity. The rest very much wanted an escape from their lives. We do not judge how they got there. We are working with parishes in Denver to build programs to care for women physically and spiritually. It would be like the place where Adele stayed."

Sarah was overcome by the generosity of these women. "What about Miss Ellie?" she said, unsuccessfully hiding her bitter tone. "What does she have to say about all of this kindness affecting her business?"

"You misjudge Miss Ellie," Mrs. Sullivan admonished her. "Who do you think is paying for all of this good work?"

A small funeral procession surrounded Kat's grave. Despite the violent threat to her life, Sarah had a small headstone made. It read,

Kat, beloved mother of Thomas

Racing Home

John refused to return Sarah to the boarding house. He was not going to let something happen to her or their baby. But even newly enlightened wagging tongues are still wagging tongues.

The wedding date was set for the next weekend.

"How do we celebrate a Quaker wedding?" asked Sarah.

"I have only attended a few when I was a lad. I remember everybody sitting in a circle, quiet for a long time. The couple stands to say simple vows. God marries us, so we don't use clergy. Members of the group, if they are moved, may stand to say something. Sometimes it is advice. Sometimes it is well-wishing."

"But I don't believe in God."

"Say your vows in a way that are meaningful to you."

"I can't promise to obey you."

"I'm not asking."

"Don't you think we can have a small wedding at Mrs. Sullivan's?" John's face opened, and deep laughter spilled out. "What's so funny?" she asked, slightly irritated.

"The whole town of Jordan came out to rescue you. They feel they own a little part of you, in a positive way. It will be a huge public outdoor wedding."

"How on earth can something like that be planned in less than a week!"

"Plan? All we have to do is say wedding, Saturday, 2:00. Everybody will be there in their Sunday best. Every picnic bench will be groaning with food. All we have to do is marry."

Sarah liked this ready-made wedding. She wondered if they could get a daguerreotype. Their flowers would be the wildflowers of fall. No need to pick a church. "Rain! What if it rains?" she poked John.

"I guess the wedding is off and we all go home," he grinned at her."

"No really."

"I have in on good faith that it will be a bright sunny day, not too hot, not too cold with a slight breeze. After what we have been through, it is the least God can give us."

Sarah's one regret was her wedding dress. "I could get a beautiful gown from Miss Ellie, but something tells me the townsfolk won't approve," she mused. Sarah headed to the boarding house. Maybe one of the girls would have a dress better suited than her calico. A second matter occupied her mind, too.

Mrs. Sullivan ran down the porch to hug her. "How are you feeling?"

"Good, good. I am a little tired sometimes. John takes one look at me and hurries me to bed like I am a child, not a full-grown woman. I get annoyed but I fall asleep like that child."

Mrs. Sullivan chuckled knowingly.

"How is Adele making out?" asked Sarah. Mrs. Sullivan had housed Adele until a job could be found.

"She is restless. She works hard and practically knocks me out of the way to finish the chores."

"I talked to Adele a couple of weeks ago about finding a position in a house. I know of a new household that could use her talents. John and I talked, and we can use some of my doctoring money to pay her."

"Wonderful! Adele can have a safe place to work. Even teach you how to use that, what do you call it? That dadburn stove?" Sarah didn't tell her she called it a lot worse than that.

Adele happened by, struggling under a large wicker basket of laundry. "Miss Sarah! Shouldn't you still be layin' in bed? Does Mr. Johnnie know you are here?"

"He gave me a key and let me out of my cage for the afternoon."

"Wa'll I be watchin' over you and making sure your baby is safe."

"Remember I told you I might find you a position in a household?"

"I sure do Dr. Sarah. I've been praying that it will come true."

"What do you think about working for us?"

Adele squealed high enough that Sarah's ears rang. "Do ya mean it? I can come work for you?"

Stay or Go?

"We'd be happy to have you."

"You can have your baby and still be Dr. Sarah." Adele stopped short. "I mean if you would let someone like me help with the baby."

"Of course, I would depend on you to help. The baby should call you Auntie Adele. Adele turned pink with pleasure.

"Why don't you come to the homestead tomorrow? You can stay in the original cabin. I'll help you decorate it, so it looks just like your own home."

"I never had a home before. I never thought I would have a baby to take care of." Adele's voice was wondrous. She wandered towards the clothesline in a dream.

"Come sit on the porch and have a cup of tea," Mrs. Sullivan invited her. "Are you going to have Maddy delivery the baby?" It hadn't occurred to Sarah to do it any other way. "Some women prefer Dr. Hancock."

"Nice as he is, I prefer a woman with sixty years of wisdom and love in her hands." Even saying this, Sarah's heart skipped a few beats at the thought of childbirth in 1882. She pushed the thought to the back of her head. Her life would not be ruled by fear. She would do anything to ensure the life of this child.

"I want to show you something." Mrs. Sullivan brought out a box, containing a rose-colored dress, and carefully displayed it for Sarah.

"What a beautiful dress!"

229

"Of course, we didn't have time to make your own wedding dress. I looked into my heart and then my trunk. I pulled out my daughter's wedding gown. I altered it to your measurements. Would you consider wearing it? Let's try it on. The princess seamed bodice had inset accordion pleats. The high neck had ecru lace. The front draped down, close to the body. A lace-trimmed bustle completed the wedding dress.

"You made this dream creation, didn't you?"

"I sewed every stitch with love for my daughter. I thought why should the dress stay in my trunk when there is a beautiful woman so close to my heart who could fill it with love?"

Sarah hugged Mrs. Sullivan as hard as she could, then pulled away to examine the dress in the mirror. It wasn't just the beautiful dress, whose color matched the rose in her cheeks that made her stare. It was a Sarah she had never seen before. Her long down-turned mouth curved up happily at the corners. Her bright hazel eyes crinkled with smile lines and shone with confidence. Her chestnut hair had grown quite long now. The last thing could not be defined as a feature but as an aura. She looked like a well-loved woman.

"Can I ask one thing," Mrs. Sullivan's voice quieted. "Would you call me Mother Sullivan?"

"It would be a great blessing, Mother Sullivan."

John must have cut that deal with the divine weatherman. Sarah awoke to a day full of the promised sunshine. The flavor of autumn perfumed the air. Trees glowed in a calliope of colors. Some trees were partly green and yellow. The aspen and fruit trees were dressed in yellow hues. Sagebrush laid a dusty green carpet.

This morning Sarah May rode to town. Tonight, Mrs. John McIntyre would return. She snuggled her hip closer to John, who nudged her with a smile. Chestnut's cheerful trot marked the significance of the day. Sarah packed her wedding dress in a neat box, tied against the dust.

Mrs. Sullivan was in her element directing staff and girls in cleaning, cooking, and preparation tasks. "Here you are, you are late!"

"We are fifteen minutes early," grinned John.

"Well, that is as good as late." She swept Sarah into the house, telling John not to come back until it was time for the wedding. John moved to kiss Sarah on the mouth, but Mrs. Sullivan intervened. "You will have plenty of time for that after the wedding."

John kept grinning. In fact, he couldn't stop smiling. What a day. What a gift. Sarah May.

Sarah was escorted to Mother Sullivan's room. She sat in front of a large mirror. "Charlotte used that mirror to get ready for her wedding too. Liza brushed, combed, and braided Sarah's chestnut hair into a French braid that framed Sarah's face and then lay curled over her left shoulder. Late blooming wild roses were placed strategically in the braid. The girls laughed and chattered. One voice rose above the crowd. "Something old, something new, something borrowed something blue!" Chaos broke out as they ensured the tradition was upheld. Sarah, enjoying the attention said, "The dress is borrowed from Mother Sullivan's daughter."

"I have my grandmother's kerchief that you can tuck in your sleeve. She embroidered it herself before coming west. That will be something old."

"What could they do for something new?" thought Sarah. She was the newest object there.

"I have something! A newly minted 1882 penny. Putting it in your shoe portends fortune." A shiny Indian head penny was placed into Sarah's slipper.

A shy girl mused her way forward. Whispering so low, the girls had to gather around to hear her. "My aunt was a bit of a wild woman. She gave me a naughty present when I was 16. I think it might be perfect today. The girl drew out a blue satin garter. The boarding house girls were shocked and thrilled at the same time. Sarah laughed, thinking of John's reaction. He'll believe he is back at Miss Ellie's. Sarah slipped the garter on just before Mother Sullivan returned to the room.

She couldn't help but compare this sisterly camaraderie, complete with a mother, to her first wedding. She could see how her own seriousness and practicality cheated her of this joyful women's ritual.

Mother Sullivan placed the bridal gown over Sarah's head. A delicate lace veil settled behind her braid. With every piece settled, and every button closed, the girls became quiet. "What, did we miss something?" Sarah turned in a circle looking for a flaw."

"You have silenced these chatterboxes," said Mother Sullivan. "They see the bride they all hope to be. Fresh, beautiful, and in love." With those words, Sarah's inner light glowed brighter. It was time to start the wedding.

John stood in the parlor, and Sarah caught her breath. It was not that he was handsome, though he was. Eschewing fancy clothes that would be out of character, he chose clothes that defined his true personality. Black pants, with a perfectly ironed crease. A starched white shirt with a disposable collar. His black leather vest covered the shirt. The collar was trimmed with a black bolo. His boots shone. He had donned a new cream-colored cowboy hat. John still had a grin on his face. Sarah detected a faint whiff of whiskey.

Great, I'll never get him to look serious during the wedding.

They linked arms and made their way down the steps. Sarah judged it a small triumph that she didn't trip. John thought so too when he pretended to let the air out of his mouth at the bottom of the steps.

Two chairs, lightly adorned with leaves and ivy, sat below the porch. Sarah gazed at most of Jordan, sitting on blankets, in carriages, on tailgates – anywhere there was room. Once again, she couldn't help but contrast this to her first wedding. She could not have found 50 people for that event. Now there were many hundreds.

The service started in silence. Sarah remembered John's words, "Look at the inner light in your heart." At first, Sarah's thoughts were confused. Events and people rushed in and out. Small nuggets of understanding began to coalesce and unite her thoughts to her life.

Her marriage elevated her thoughts to a new understanding. White Buffalo's advice about finding a different path confused her in the past. Now her way was clear. She and John led the way. John carried their baby, and Sarah held Mia's heart. This new family would forge the path of the future. Maybe there would be even more babies. Certainly, there would be heartache. Sarah, at last, understood what it meant to bond two people together.

John cleared his throat, startling Sarah. She realized the length of her reverie. "You were thinking so long I figured you were talking yourself out of it," he whispered.

"Hardly."

They faced each other. Trying to mimic the seriousness of the ceremony was fruitless. Their smiles were broad, and their hazel eyes crinkled with happiness.

John's love was evident with every word:

In the presence of God and these friends, I take thee Sarah May to be my wife, I promise with Divine Assistance to be unto thee a loving and faithful husband as long as we shall live.

Sarah's heart swelled, answering:

In the presence of all that binds and all these friends, I take thee John McIntyre to be my husband, promising to be unto thee a faithful wife as long as we shall live.

Though it was a non-Quaker tradition, John slipped the golden topaz ring out of his vest pocket. The sun glinted through the ring, glowing on the gem that settled on her finger. It remained there for the rest of her life. Bill stood before the couple to read the Quaker Marriage Certificate.

"In the presence of the light and love of family and friends, I take thee to be my beloved, promising to be a loving and faithful partner. I ask you to be none other than yourself. I promise to cherish and delight in your spirit and individuality, and face life's challenges with patience and humor, respect our differences, and to nurture our growth. This commitment is made in love, kept in faith, lived in hope, and made eternally new."

"In celebration of this commitment, we set our hands," finished Bill, gesturing towards the marriage certificate.

John and Sarah signed; Sarah was relieved she only made one small blotch.

Bill continued: "And as members of a loving community , we set our hands in caring witness to this union. Any person present may sign as a witness to this union."

At the end of the day, it took six feet of brown wrapping paper to hold the signatures. Sarah was particularly charmed to see Tommy's rough scrawl, as well illiterate scribbles of other children. Curiously, there was also a dog print.

"Where in the ceremony does the bride get kissed?" asked Sarah with pretended insult. John wrapped one arm around her waist, and the other around her shoulder, kissing her deeply and bending her backward. The crowd cheered when it was apparent John's kiss rendered Sarah dizzy and weak-kneed.

Sarah wanted to dance at their wedding. Nothing fancy, but another small thing she missed on her first go-round. They moved to an open area where two fiddlers and a singer started the song. Sarah knew the music after the first few notes. John held her close as the song began.

I see leaves of green, red roses too,

The melody may have been a bit off-key, but Sarah believed it was the best cover of any Louis Armstrong rendition. The guests were hushed.

John fulfilled Sarah's last wish with the presence of a photographer. Instead of the formal sitting pose, they posed with the stance of John holding Sarah while they danced.

The autumn breeze danced along with the newlyweds. Time stopped; Sarah, beautiful in her wedding gown, and John's heart was finally satisfied. They danced after the music ended, unaware of anything but their love .Bill stood for the first toast: "John and I grew up and attended school together. We fought constantly. I am proud to say I gave John his first bloody nose. I am humbled to say that he gave me my first black eye." The crowd tittered. The older adults remembered the boy's scuffles. John's future as the son of a landowner was assured. My prospects were less so. Ainsley McIntyre hired me at the age of 14, teaching both of us to run a horse farm. John never treated me like a hired hand. As far as he was concerned, we were equal partners. That is still how it is. He says we are partners in crime, not his help. Sometimes I forget that John is not my brother. When I first laid my eyes on this feisty bride Sarah, I thought, maybe this is the one. Through some trials by fire, John finally had sense enough to marry the best thing that has happened in his life. At least the best thing after me." John laughed. "I give one piece of advice." John sat straighter, turning his ear, to better absorb his friend's advice. "Don't try to solve all of your problems at once; life is complicated. Problems can be complicated. Sometimes it is better to let a problem lie, kick it around a bit before you try to fix it."

Mrs. Sullivan stood next. "One day a suspicious and bedraggled woman came to my doorstep looking for shelter. Now I love Sarah as a daughter. Miracles can happen when you open your hearts. That is my advice: keep open hearts, and love will continue to pour in."

It took a long time, but even shy Adele spoke softly. "Mr. Johnnie and Dr. Sarah saved my life twice. Once when I was sick, and now when I needed a real job. Thank you."

Sarah thought she knew John well, but the appreciation from the townspeople imparted a long history. Thank you's for John helping rebuild a burnt cabin with the addition of a Shaker chair to make it home. The storyteller imparted the wisdom to build a home in their hearts and fill it with beautiful things. Others spoke of John's willingness and nonjudgmental ear in times of crisis, urging the couple to listen to each other in the same way.

A group of men, maybe more than a bit tipsy, recounted their tale. John led a group of hunters on their annual quest for elk meat. The elk proved elusive. John found sign – elk rubs, elk footprints, elk droppings, but could never find the actual elk. He bugled, but the answers seem to be scattered all over the valley. "John led us up one draw and down the other, we crossed creeks, scrambled over boulders, and we were dog-tired around dark. We called it a day, looking forward to camp, whiskey, and bed, in that order. As we stepped into camp, John stood silent. A small herd of five elk were grazing right by our tents. The moral of the story is that you don't have to travel the long hard path. Your answer may be right at home."

John grinned at the stories directed at him. Humble Sarah blushed from the gratitude from the community. It amazed her that she had touched so many lives in such a short time. Sarah was astonished to see Miss Ellie rise to speak. She did not know the brothel owner had attended the wedding. "Sarah, you have touched my life in ways you can't imagine. I see people are more than what you can get out of them. They have hopes and dreams. Maybe I can be blessed enough to help them on their way."

The congratulations continued until the smell of the food overpowered the words. The picnic broke out. John and Sarah strolled around the group to talk to their guests. The greetings seemed random, but Sarah realized that they were purposefully zigzagging through the crowd.

"Why are we going this way?"

"Because Mrs. Jones makes the best-fried chicken in town."

Sarah caught on quickly. "I take it Mrs. Johnson makes the best chocolate cake?"

"Good enough to make me cry."

The wedding party broke apart as chore time arrived.

Sarah poked John in the ribs. "Look!" Bill and Adele sat at a picnic table talking. It looked like they had been there for a while. Bill looked engaged while Adele's cheeks flamed pink. John bemused, "Maybe we have the start of something."

They drove home in the light buggy before the party ended. John pulled Sarah into the barn without taking care of Chestnut. Sarah, well-schooled in 'livestock first', felt confused.

"What about Chestnut?"

"I want you to see something." He led her to the last small stall. There, laying on a blanket of straw was a black and white dog, with a litter of wriggling puppies, all competing for mom's supply of milk.

"Puppies!" she opened the stall door, plopping down on the straw, wedding dress, and all. They immediately swarmed to her. She tried to count them, but their constant movement made it impossible.

"There are eight puppies. Mom is from Mr. Sawyer from two ranches over."

"Do we keep them all?" Sarah felt a little overwhelmed.

"You get to keep the pick of the litter."

"You expect me to find only one that I love the most?" Just then a tiny puppy made its way to Sarah, licking her into a giggle. John thought this puppy might be a contender.

"What kind of dogs are they?"

"I guess you call them cow dogs. They help with herding and things like that."

Sarah disentangled herself from the pack. She rushed into John's arms. "Thank you, what a perfect present. You can go back into the cabin now; I will stay with the puppies." John changed her mind with a sensual kiss, reminding them both of the wedding night to come.

"I guess I can't stay out here anyway. I have something for you."

They passed Bill caring for Chestnut. "Hope you guys hold it down tonight, I need some sleep." The ribbing met with laughter as Bill lived a quarter mile down the road.

Sarah led John to the kitchen table. A large box, wrapped in brown paper stood in the middle. He scooted it to the edge, surprised at the weight. "What do you have in here, a lifetime supply of horseshoes?" Sarah danced around, eager for the big reveal. John slowly tore off the paper, intentionally teasing her. When he eyed the gift, he yanked the rest off post-haste. In the box sat a full set of new law books. Sarah...." He trailed off as he pulled them out one by one. He flipped through the pages of a tome.

Stay or Go?

"I thought now that you have a wife who liked working in the home and land you love since the time you were born, you would want to study law again."

John pulled Sarah onto his lap, and they rocked in his Faither's chair. He carried Sarah to the bedroom. They sealed their union with a night of tender, and sometimes raucous lovemaking they hoped Bill couldn't hear.

Day one of married life began with the first day of 40 hours of work for every hour of play.

Work assumed a different timbre when performed with union and love rather than Kat's bitterness. John, Sarah, Bill, and Adele sat after a satisfying breakfast. They discussed sharing chores, which were divided by skill and time. Adele, wanting to prove her worth, kept volunteering for the lion's share of the load.

"Before we start," said Bill, "let's not forget we do not have to solve everything today. Nothing is written in stone. We have to work together." John and Sarah agreed with the advice he shared at the wedding. Bill and Adele would get the water in the morning. The men wanted to build a cistern, bringing running water closer to the home. Mother Sullivan had volunteered to teach the women to cook. Adele cooked hearty meals already, but said, "Iffen I learn to cook good all of our tummies will be happier." Adele begged the group to be allowed to plant a garden. "I always wanted a garden of my own. When I was wee, my ma had a garden, and I helped her pull the weeds and water it every day." Who would deny a chore that would bring such happiness into Adele's life?

"I guess you get the chickens, Sarah," said John. I'll build a coop this week. Adele will have to clean the coop until the baby is born."

Sarah offered to walk the horses to the pasture with John. It would be a special time for the married couple to be outdoors together, as well as healthy exercise during the pregnancy.

The only protested decision was laundry. Adele insisted she could manage laundry for four. Sarah pictured Adele struggling under Mother Sullivan's wicker basket and put her foot down. "Adele, it is too much to do laundry for four people. Think of how much more there will be when the baby comes, diapers and all." They reached a compromise by sending out the laundry. Adele insisted on personally washing the baby's clothes. That settled that issue.

The homestead prospered under the hard work of John and Bill. Sarah received payment in many different forms. Some paid in cash. She received many chickens, some live, some plucked and ready for the oven. Eggs often overwhelmed the pantry. Adele looked for creative ways to serve them. Sacks of flour and sugar, wild game, and home-canned jellies marked payment in full. Often a man would offer a day's work- always welcome.

The day after John finished the chicken coop, he surprised Sarah with a flat of little chicks. "You are trying to trick me into keeping the chickens!" The little peepers were so soft and adorable that Sarah had to drag herself away from them to do her other chores. Sarah hovered over the momma dog and her pups. She changed her mind daily about which one to choose. The small group settled into a happy routine. The homestead lost some of its rough edges, becoming more self-sufficient.

242

Sarah knew John liked to sing while he worked. She heard many old songs like "Cockles and Mussels," "Goober peas," and "Swanee River." His pleasant baritone filled the barn, calming the animals.

One day, Sarah was feeding the chickens and heard a different sound. A familiar rhythmic thumping and clapping. Sarah peeked around the barn door and saw John enthusiastically stomp his heavy boots twice on the floor, then clap. He sang a familiar song but needed to substitute many words when he didn't know the lyrics.

"John!" He startled, then looked a bit sheepish. "What song is that?" Sarah had a suspicion.

"It's from your smartphone. Remember when I listened to the songs when I waited for you on the mountain." The men called themselves Queen, but I didn't see a Queen on the picture. I thought it was like calling a horse Queenie."

"You like Freddie Mercury! You have excellent taste in music," Sarah laughed. "I love Freddie Mercury, too. I'll teach it to you." She showed him how to keep the rhythm while singing the lyrics. They danced around the barn, finally collapsing on stacked hay bales, out of breath from the singing, dancing, and laughing.

John laid his head back. I dinna think there was such fun as dancin' to Queen Freddie Mercury. Sarah pulled her sweaty hair out of her face; her wide mouth smiled ear to ear. "Why did they call themselves Queen?"

"I don't know for sure, but I think it was because Freddie Mercury was a homosexual."

John drew back, "What?"

"In 2022, it is OK to live openly as homosexuals. Men who love men, women who loved women, and other sexual choices."

"You must have had a lot of homosexuals," he said with distaste.

"I bet the numbers are the same as now. What happens here when someone is even suspected of being a homosexual?"

"If they are lucky they are killed, if they are not lucky, much worse."

"So, wouldn't you do anything to hide the fact that you are gay?"

"Gay?"

"A modern term for homosexual."

"I guess that's true."

"There are so many talented, creative gay people in our entertainment industry."

"I'd have a hard time getting used to it."

Sarah poked him hard in the arm with her finger. "They would have a hard time getting used to you."

Leaves began falling as autumn matured. Sarah was fully into her second trimester. Like her pregnancy with Mia, her libido roared into high gear. She lay awake in bed waiting for John to finish reading his law book. He would tiptoe in the room, trying not to wake her. Instead, he found her awake and not-so-patiently waiting.

One day Sarah tracked John to a distant pasture. He looked at her grinning face. "Och no! I hid here to get a wee bit o' rest. Ye still found me. One more time this week and it will fall off."

"I doubt that," she said, unbuttoning his pants.

They scarred Bill for life. Sarah taught John the music and dance for Twist and Shout. The lessons rocketed out of control. Bill found them dishabille in the barn hay. He never walked into the barn again without whistling loudly from fifty yards away.

In bed, at night they dreamed about the baby. John touched her belly in circular movements. When his hand coincided with a kick, excitement showed on his face. "Look at that!' he said in amazement, no matter how many times it happened. "A kick that strong means it is a boy."

"Maddy says I am carrying low, so it is a girl."

"What does a midwife with sixty years' experience know?" He leaned to talk directly to her belly. "I know my wee baby is Scottish, no?"

Mother Sullivan, Adele, and Sarah were secretive on John's birthday. They gathered after breakfast and shooed the men away early. John received no respite from work, despite his special day. His reward was served at dinner. A scrumptious meal cooked by all three women. "Don't eat too much," Sarah admonished anxiously.

"Who could stop eating a dinner like this?" The reason for her anxiety was presented after the meal. Sarah balanced a three-layer chocolate cake, placing it on the table. "I made every bit of it myself."

"The woman who almost burned this cabin down?"

"I can take the cake back and give it to the squirrels."

"Oh, no. What a grand birthday present. I'll share tiny pieces with the rest of you, and you will be lucky for it." John ate until his stomach distended uncomfortably. Even then, he got up in the middle of the night for more.

Dr. Sarah climbed on Clover riding into town three days a week. There was precious little time before taking her pregnancy leave. Maddy and Dr. Hancock agreed she could no longer ride after seven months. Sarah concurred, knowing her previous history of premature labor. Dr. Hancock took on another apprentice to cover her absence.

The modern immunization supply was depleted. Sarah figured that since most of the town's children were immunized, it would prevent illness and death from common diseases for almost ten years. One box held all that was left of the antibiotics. Sarah learned to use old remedies, only administering the antibiotics sparingly.

Miss Ellie visited one afternoon. "I'm out of those miracle pills, can I buy some more?"

"When I sold you the last batch, I told you that was the end of them. You needed to make them last."

Miss Ellie stomped off angrily. Sarah felt angry too. She felt torn deciding who would get the precious medicine and who would flirt with death.

Who am I to decide these things?

Through this idyllic fall, Sarah caught shimmers of Mia. Playing with the twin foals. Wriggling with the puppies. She was sure Mia urged her to choose the favorite black and white pup who was so eager to kiss. Mia pronounced the puppy's name Billy, and so it was.

Maddy checked her health every week. Sarah enjoyed their time together. They sat on the porch drinking tea. "you only have a few months to go, are you thinking about when your time comes?"

It was time to talk to Maddy about her terror. "I am frightened beyond belief about giving birth. Not typically frightened, but desperately so."

"Every woman fears childbirth."

"I think I have an abnormal fear. I don't know how I can bear it."

"Why do you feel like this, child?"

Sarah hesitated, not sure how to explain modern-world obstetrics. "Where I come from, there is a treatment, sort of a magical remedy. It makes childbirth not so painful. I used it when I had Mia."

"Can you use it again?"

"No, I can only use it back there."

Maddy shook her head, not understanding nor believing. "Do you have any plans to help with your fear?"

"I want John to be in the room with me."

"That is unconventional."

"I need the strength of both of us to deliver the child."

"What does John think?"

"That he loves me and will do anything to help me through my time. I don't think I could bear losing another child."

Maddy made no false promises, but patted Sarah's hand. "I find that praying to God to provide strength is always helpful."

Sarah twisted her lips.

Sarah was washing breakfast dishes when she first heard it. Adele screamed at the top of her lungs.

"Dr. Sarah, Mr. John fell and is hurt bad. Bill says bring your bag." She grabbed her bag, running as fast as the baby allowed. John lay on the ground grimacing. Bill held rags against John's calf with as much strength as he could summon. The blood-saturated rag after rag.

"What happened!" John's teeth clenched against the pain, so Bill answered. "He was fixing a hinge on the hayloft window and fell off the ladder. He fell against that bow saw."

"Adele, take Clover and get Dr. Hancock as fast as you can." Adele flew out of the barn.

"John, I have to look at your leg." Bill removed the rags; Sarah saw a jagged laceration. In some places, the saw cut through skin, muscle, and bits of white bone. The field flooded with blood. Sarah took muslin out of the bag, wrapped it around the leg. Then she inserted a small piece of wood in the ends, and twisted until the blood flow slowed. She was satisfied the tourniquet was slowing the bleeding. But that was only a stop-gap measure. She then packed the wound with rags. She elevated his leg above his heart and then wrapped the leg firmly.

OK. She thought, - emergency nurse mode. Airway – check. Breathing – check. Circulation. Pulse, a concerning 112 beats per minute. The tourniquet slowed the leg bleeding, but she had done everything she could. Sarah willed Dr. Hancock to speed his way here. She needed to check for other injuries. Pressing on his abdomen," she asked, "Does anything hurt here?" He shook his head. She checked his head finding no lumps. "Can you tell me your name?"

"Why the hell are you asking me my name?"

"I'm trying to figure out your injuries."

"John McIntyre," he gritted.

"Who is the president?" That was an automatic question, but fruitless; not knowing the answer herself.

"The president! Who the hell cares? Chester Arthur!"

Sarah noted swelling over one clavicle, suspecting a fracture. The blood began to saturate the bandage and she tightened the tourniquet. Bill helped her add another tight layer over the dressing. Sarah saw John's ankle rapidly swell and bruise. A sprain or a fracture?

Dr. Hancock arrived at the barn, pulling his horse to a stop so quickly it reared in its traces.

"How did you get here so fast?" asked Sarah, even though it seemed like hours.

"I was already in town." Sarah apprised him of John's injuries. They needed to stop the bleeding before the tourniquet caused tissue damage.

"Adele," he ordered, bring me all the tea you have. The tannic acid will help a little."

Sarah set out the doctor's surgical kit. She gave John a dose of morphine before they began. "Bill, please bring a basin of warm water and rags. We need to clean John's wound before we sew it up. Sarah poured the water mixed with tea over the wound, as Dr. Hancock stitched, trying to flush anything lodged in his leg.

Even with Dr. Hancock's skill and Sarah's competent assistance, it took over an hour to sew the tissues to stem the bleeding to a slow trickle while releasing the tourniquet.

Adele sat at John's head, keeping up an unending chatter to distract him from his pain. With John's ankle wrapped and his clavicle in a sling, he could be moved. Bill rounded up neighboring men. Using a makeshift stretcher, They lifted him into the cabin bedroom. John lay quiet, as white as a ghost, fear written on his face.

Dr. Hancock talked to Sarah outside the cabin. "Do have any of those antibiotics left?"

"I do." She had organized a stash of medications and immunizations to treat a future family illness. Call it selfish, or call it survival, she had the right to protect her family.

"I worry about lockjaw with that rusty blade."

"I immunized John against tetanus this summer."

"There is no doubt the wound will become infected. I hope your antibiotics work."

"I have three different kinds. I will give him two that are good for wounds. I don't think the third will help much; it is more for pneumonia.

"If anyone can pull John through, it will be you. I'll be back in the morning.

Stay or Go?

In the cabin, Sarah ordered, "Bill, please get some cold water for John from the spring. Adele, could you make some weak tea? A little caffeine might boost his system. We must replace some of the fluids he lost. We have some jars of Mother Sullivan's broth. Let's heat that, too."

She took his pulse – 120. He felt cold and clammy, in early stages of shock. She kept his legs elevated with quilts tucked around his body. John drank the small sips of tea that she offered every five minutes.

"How bad is it?"

Sarah hedged. "Your clavicle is broken, but that will heal nicely in about six weeks.?

"How bad is it?"

"We think your foot…"

"Sarah, stop! You know what I mean."

"It's bad. Part of the saw slashed the muscle to the bone."

"Will I walk again?"

Sarah reassured him. "Of course. It will take time and therapy, but you will walk. Maybe with a limp though."

"How are we going to keep the homestead going?"

"I am sure you and Bill can make a plan when you are a little better." Sarah was glad he occupied his mind with walking and working. She didn't want him to think about the deadly infection he would first have to overcome.

Sarah stayed with him the entire night. Her intensive care brought John through the initial shock. By morning his skin felt dry and moist. His pulse beat at a more reassuring 102.

Mother Sullivan rode in with Dr. Hancock. After looking at Sarah, she took over. "Adele, let Sarah sleep in your bed for a while. She addressed a bruised-eyed Sarah. "You have to rest. Your baby depends on you. I will take care of John."

Dr. Hancock deferred removing the bandage this morning, giving the wounds more time to stop seeping blood. John's normal temperature reassured him that an infection had not started. Sarah's ministrations pulled him through his shock.

"Are you in pain?"

"I didn't want to say it in front of Sarah, but it hurts like a son of a bitch."

"You were too sick to get morphine last night; we can give you small doses today."

"Is Sarah telling me the truth? I will walk again?"

"The cut is severe. It sliced through quite a bit of muscle. I sewed it as carefully as I could. Some of the work was rough because of the bleeding. I am expecting an infection; much depends on your ability to fight it."

"Sarah didn't tell me about an infection," John said, piqued.

"Sarah kept you alive last night," admonished the doctor. "You need to be grateful for her skills. Take the medicine that Sarah gives you. Drink the meat broth that Mrs. Sullivan makes. It has high-quality protein and salt to build you up. I will come by in the morning to change the bandage."

Bill stuck his head in the cabin later in the morning. "Is the boss awake?"

"Do you need to bother him about work?" bristled Mrs. Sullivan.

"I have news that will let him rest better." Bill entered the bedroom. "Jesus Christ, I have seen better-looking drowned rats."

"Damn, not you again."

"Why'd you have to pull a stunt like that? If you needed a day off, just say it." John had no retort. "I know you are laying here worrying yourself sick about the homestead. I thought I'd talk to you about the plan. Mrs. Sullivan and the church ladies can manage the cooking and cleaning. That will free Adele to help me. She already knows what to do. You know that gal is one hard worker."

"There is enough work out there for three men, not one man and a girl."

"It seems there are a lot of men out there who feel like they owe you a favor. You have been sticking your nose in their business so long that they think you need a payback. Joe Robinson came over this morning and said he organized a work crew. A man

254

will come every day to help with the work until you are on your feet. Though why they would help an ugly cuss like you is beyond me."

Relief washed over John. There were many things he could bear; losing his father's homestead wasn't one of them. "I'd say thank you, but your head would swell too big to go back through that door."

"I gotta go help Adele in the barn."

John caught something in Bill's tone. "Are you getting sweet on that little lady?"

"I just may be."

Sarah woke with a start, realizing she had slept until evening. "What kind of doctor are you? I've been needing some of your special doctoring all day," said John when she reached his bedside.

"How are you feeling?"

"I feel like a stupid man who stepped off a ladder and now is helpless in bed while others do his work."

"It was an accident."

"How am I supposed to take care of my beautiful pregnant wife?"

"Your beautiful pregnant doctor wife can take care of you for once."

John pulled her head down with his good arm, kissing her. "I'm sorry. I'll be better before you know it."

"Things can change in a split instant when you least expect it." She averted her gaze so he wouldn't see her thoughts of Mia. Her ruse didn't work. He lifted her jaw. "This is not at all like Mia."

But wasn't it?

Dr. Hancock removed the dressing. Sarah poured water steeped in tea while the doctor eased the soaked bandage. The wound bled in several places but could be controlled with light pressure. The skin appeared red and angry. The swelling pulled at the stitches. John examined the wound. "I guess it is what I expected." The laceration looked like what Sarah and Dr. Hancock expected, too. The body's reaction to an injury would be to send fluids filled with cells that fight infection. Thus, the swelling and redness. Sarah dabbed the crusty drainage. Despite being given morphine before the work, John responded by sharp intakes of his breath. "Easy as she goes, girl."

Sarah nodded but continued until the wound looked meticulously clean. "I have antibiotic ointment for the incision lines. It's not very strong, but anything might help."

The doctor said, "Keep up with the antibiotics and pain medicine. You know what to do, Sarah. I'll be back in the morning."

Mother Sullivan drew Sarah out to the kitchen. "John, you rest now so I can take care of Sarah. Come on, honey. You need to eat." Sarah began to protest. "If you can't eat for yourself, fine, but you must eat for your baby." Sarah spooned the food from the plate into her mouth, not caring to identify the contents. "Instead of telling me the bad, tell me the good that can happen." Sarah sighed, "John will undoubtedly get an infection. The antibiotics and his general good health will fight it. The wound will begin to heal. His clavicle will quickly mend, as will the sprained, not fractured ankle. He can get out of bed within a week; I can start physical therapy. He will use a crutch in another week, though physical therapy might take months. He will regain his strength to walk, though with a limp. The injury will not impede his ability to work or enjoy life."

"That sounds like a wonderful path for John to take, don't you?" Instead of only thinking the worst, there was a realistic way through the accident. Sarah felt comforted. "The prayer chain is already on their knees 24 hours a day for John. I know you have a curious take on religion, but isn't there a way you can ask for help?" Sarah could only remember her sore knees and desperate thoughts, helpless to prevent Mia's death. Latching on to the idea of John's potential recovery would follow a positive path. Sarah sat in the room with John all day. They talked about everything but the accident. One favorite topic included naming the baby. They discussed serious names like John, Robert, and Ainsley. John insisted he also liked Haggis, Bean, and Murdock. He argued they did not need to spend time on girls' names because the only outcome of this pregnancy would be a baby boy. When Sarah told him that the man's DNA determined the sex of the baby, he triumphed. "See! Of course, we will have a boy!"

"Does that mean I will never get a little girl?"

"After two or three boys, I'll let you have your girl."

"Thanks," she said dryly. But to humor her, they talked about girls' names. Ainsley came up again, being a name for a boy or a girl. Anna and Claire struck their fancy. John needled her by insisting he loved the names Matilda and Morag.

The next dressing change discouraged all, but it was not unexpected. The infection set in; the clear drainage turned yellow. The war between John's health and the bacteria began. John ran a slight fever of 100.1 degrees, Sarah encouraged him to drink even more fluids as he ate light meals. Worrying about leg clots and pneumonia, she decided he needed to get out of bed. After a hefty close of morphine, Bill and Adele helped him sit in a chair.

John, looking for a way to distract himself from the pain, asked Sarah to talk about the future. 'Do you know anything about guns?"

"Very little, thinking about the gun that lay at the lake. Only how much more powerful guns, artillery, and missiles became during wars."

"Wars! Tell me about wars."

"I don't want to talk about such terrible things when you are trying to get better."

"No, it is like studying history in reverse. I really want to know."

Sarah capitulated. "The Civil War was the deadliest of all the American wars. More Americans died in the Civil War than in all the other wars combined. There may have been some small wars around the turn of the century, but I am not sure. They called the next war the Great War. The cause is confusing, nothing definitive like the Civil War. It seemed like a lot of countries, especially Germany, became very militaristic. Everybody wanted to expand their borders. One thing I remember most was trench warfare. Both sides would dig deep trenches, then in between would be a bombed-out area full of barbed wire. They called it No Man's Land. They led charges by leaving the trenches and trying to advance further into this land. Once you were out of the trench, you were a sitting duck. The other horrendous deed was the use of mustard gas. It was called chemical warfare. When the men would breathe it, their lungs melted. John looked horrified. In this war, not only the soldiers were killed, maybe around 10 million of them. But a huge number of civilians died - maybe 7 million.

John interrupted. "Million? Seventeen million?"

"Yes, Million. Is this enough? Do we have to talk about war anymore?"

"Who won?"

"Does anybody win a war like that? The United States, Great Britain, and France won. The most important thing was that Germany was crushed."

"Why was that important?"

Stay or Go?

"Do you want to keep talking about this? Let's talk about Paradise. A place called Hawaii.

"Where is Hawaii?"

"It is a series of small islands in the South Pacific. It is heaven on earth. Volcanic mountains, blue skies, warm ocean, palm trees, fragrant flowers, gentle breezes. I have never been there, but I wish I could go. I guess that is out of the question now."

Sarah tried to turn the subject to Hawaii, but John pushed her on.

"So, the US joined a war in Europe and fought a second war in the Pacific. They used modern warfare with destroyer ships, planes, jets, bombs, and all sorts of terrible machines of death. The Navajo Code talkers added an interesting element. John quizzed her about the Indians with their unbreakable language, fascinated.

"In the end, Germany was crushed again. But not before they carried out a horrific genocide. They targeted Jews as an inferior race and systematically took their businesses, houses, and made them live in fenced ghettos. They were starved and dehumanized and shipped in cattle cars on trains to these camps. There they were mass exterminated by poisonous gas. I saw moving pictures of starvation, disease, and death. In the end, 5,000,000 Jews were killed. I think that if God could not answer the prayers of those suffering people, who certainly prayed with every fiber of their soul, he either does not exist or is very evil indeed." I prayed with every fiber of my soul for Mia, she drifted off.

John now understood another key to Sarah's spirit.

John's infection see-sawed over the next few days. In the morning, his temperature rose to 102. Purulent drainage crusted over his laceration. Sarah administered fluids, acetaminophen, and changed the dressing. She added the third antibiotic on the off chance it would work. John slept most of the afternoon. By evening his temperature dropped. Sarah entertained him with stories of books from the future. To Kill a Mockingbird enamored him; she retold the story in detail. The next morning proved worse than the last. The entire wound shone fiery red. Sutures broke open from the swelling. Sarah admitted to herself that the antibiotics failed. John alone needed to fight the infection.

Mother Sullivan implored Sarah to take a break, but she refused. She let others take care of Mia in her fight for life. This was her battle to fight hand in hand with John. She bathed him in cool water with a little alcohol. Holding his head, he could sip water and broth. Maddy visited with a poultice that Sarah gladly applied, hoping the next morning's dressing change would bring better news.

John slept longer, often waking only long enough to drink. One evening Sarah propped him up slightly, his eyes bright with fever. "Tell me about Hawaii."

No more talk of soldiers and machines. Thinking of every movie about Hawaii, she painted a picture of paradise. She appealed to his senses, from the smell of the salty ocean to the grainy black sand under his feet on the beaches. Closing his eyes, he fell asleep with a small smile.

The next day morning found that Maddy's poultice didn't work. Sarah opened the next morning to find angry red lines streaking up John's leg. Her stomach clenched. She left the dressing open for Dr. Hancock. John was confused. Dr. Hancock made short work of his exam. "Sarah, we are at the end of the road. We have to amputate his leg to save his life." Sarah knew amputation was not the answer. He was septic; the infection had traveled to his blood.

"John, I'm sorry, the only thing we can do is take your leg, it is your only chance."

Those words snapped John out of his confusion. "No! Never!" he shouted with a strength he hadn't shown for days. "I'll not do it. I can beat this infection; you can't saw off my leg." Sarah knelt next to his side. "Sarah, I won't do it, I won't."

"John, John calm down. We'll leave your leg alone." He laid back, breathing heavily. "I can't leave you and our baby."

"I have one idea; I don't know if I can even get there."

"The archway?"

"There is an antibiotic and some other medicines that go right into your blood. It may be the only chance we have."

"Can you get through again?"

"I don't know. I must try. I'll make a bargain with you. I'll get through the archway, and you fight this son-of-a-bitch infection with every cell in your body." John's fevered lips met Sarah's cool ones.

Outside the cabin, Dr. Hancock said, "I can't tell you I understand anything that is happening. Medicine in your blood? An archway?"

"I know. You must have faith that we have a plan, the only plan to save his life. No matter what," she said pointing her finger at the doctor, "no matter what, we are not going to amputate John's leg. The infection is in his blood now; an amputation is not going to help. It would just kill him faster."

"When will you have the medicine?"

"Tonight," she said with determination. Sarah had no time to dress in modern clothing. This was a survival mission. Without asking any questions, Mother Sullivan found a pair of men's pants and a flannel shirt that could be tied around Sarah's belly. The only boots were the clumsy black leather ones that Mack stocked. She prepared a knapsack of extra clothes, food, and water.

As she rode, off, she called to Bill. "Some problems can't wait."

John smiled faintly when he saw her costume as she entered the room to say goodbye.

He whispered something, and she had to bend low to hear. "Name him Ainsley, will you? Ainsley John McIntyre."

"I am not going to name our daughter any such thing. We have a deal mister. I expect you to keep your part of it." She kissed him fiercely then strode out to the familiar path. It was cold; the trail was often covered with snow. Sarah's determination overcame the obstacles. The weight of the baby slowed her somewhat, but she made the trip in under three hours.

Pulling herself over the last ridge, she looked for the archway. She knew it wouldn't be obvious and might not be open at all. Trudging back and forth, fear crept into her heart when the archway did not appear. White Buffalo could not be her guide. This was her path to solve. Out of breath, she sat. She compared Mia's and John's desperate situations. This outcome was going to be different. Her heart beat fast. The baby kicked, high under her diaphragm. Then, as if to remind her they were in it together, began to hiccup. Sarah joined energy with her baby to focus her thoughts. Her life now centered on John in 1882. The archway energy distinguished the pull from the past rather than the future. The baby belonged to John, so another power tugged behind her. What did Sarah have to catapult her into the future? She focused on the Vancomycin. It held the one connection to 2022. She needed Vancomycin. She pictured getting it at Joe's pharmacy and buying the needed supplies. She felt Jane and Joe hug her, happy to see her again. They shared the joy of her pregnancy. The energy shifted, and the archway opened.

The trip to Saratoga took place exactly as she imagined it. It was a little harder to catch a ride into town because of her strange clothing. She looked a bit like a homeless person. She didn't smell, so that helped. As the woman dropped her off at Joe's pharmacy, Sarah ran in.

"Joe! I need help again!" He looked up, immediately texting Jane. "Get here quick; it's Sarah."

"Jesus Christ Sarah, look at you."

"Joe, my husband is septic. I need some Vancomycin, steroids, IV supplies, and anything else you can think of."

Joe pulled her into the side room. "Are you OK? Are you safe?"

"I am safe, but my husband isn't. He had a terrible accident, and his wound became infected. The oral antibiotics didn't work; now he is septic. Can you get me what I need? Time is critical. He is dying." Her breath caught in her throat.

"Sit right here. Jane will be here in a second. I'll tell her to bring you something to eat." He ran out already calling the hospital to get the needed supplies.

"I need two stethoscopes and blood pressure cuffs." Sarah had only a few minutes to look around, to get the feel of what used to be her home. From her room, she watched cars drive through the streets. The speed limit was only 35 mph, yet it seemed like they were flying. There were so many people in this modern small town. The shelves were filled with over-the-counter remedies. She wondered if this store could remotely stack up against Mack's.

Jane rushed in, and the two friends fell into each other's arms. Jane immediately pulled away. "Sarah May you are pregnant!"
"It is Mrs. Sarah May McIntyre to you I'll have you know."

"Oh, Sarah, I am so happy for you. Why did you come back? What are you wearing?"

My husband has been in an accident. He's injured and is septic. Getting him IV Vancomycin is our only hope."

Jane said, "Joe messaged me and is getting everything together as fast as he can. How about you? What do you need?"

"That sandwich and Coke look good."

Jane pulled out an old picture, a daguerreotype. "Is this you? I have looked everywhere for proof that you are OK in 1882."

Sarah looked at the happy couple, dancing at their wedding. "It is me and my husband in happier times.

"I'll get you some clothes that are better suited for your trip back."

Sarah said with her mouth full of hamburger, "I wear a size seven boot, get two pairs."

"Do you need anything, like modern, to take back with you?"

Sarah only thought for a second. "I have everything I need at home." In less than two hours Sarah was dressed and loaded with a new backpack.

"Will I ever see you again?" Jane asked once more.

This time Sarah knew for certain. "No, I will be staying."

The antibiotics rode lightly in her backpack. The baby became restless though. Striding up the mountain, a cramp began in her lower back, spreading to the front of her belly. Early labor signaled disaster on both sides of the timeline. She drank large amounts of water. The contractions stayed mild and irregular. Sarah rested every 20 minutes or so. Her actions managed her symptoms. Mirror Lake signaled the halfway point. She planned a longer rest here. Squatting at the lake's edge to fill her water bottle, a sharp contraction encompassed her belly. It left her sick and panting. Come on little baby, not now. Just a bit longer and Maddy can help us.

Sarah lay on the same rock from the night she almost left. Tears started in her eyes; she would not give in to them. She promised to protect this child no matter what. Calming herself, she used yoga relaxation techniques to relax every part of her body. The contractions faded into a nagging backache. How long can I hold off? I still must go halfway up a mountain and descend it. Sarah found a walking stick-sized branch. After a long drink of water, she resumed her hike. When the trail was easy, the contractions almost stopped. When she was forced to climb, they came back with a vengeance. Many times, Sarah had to perch precariously on a rock, waiting for a contraction to subside. She made it to the lake, with the canoe still tethered by its rope. Mike's gun lay on the rock where it had been dropped. That was another lifetime ago. Then she wanted no more. Now she wanted everything, her baby's life, her husband's love, and her place in her community. The canoe paddled awkwardly, not because of Sarah's lack of skills, but because of her need to stop with each contraction. She refilled her bottle with the icy lake water, again trying to relax. This time the contractions didn't abate. Sarah thought grimly, "How long does labor last for a second-time mom? Maybe six hours. Of course, much shorter in the case of a premature baby. She had been in labor for at least three hours. At 28 weeks their child had little chance of survival in 1882. But nothing was hopeless. Giving up because of a modern medical statistic was not an option. Sarah stood awkwardly, holding onto the trees reaching the archway or rather where the entrance used to be. *Oh my God, it is closed now.* Panic rose in her throat. It had to be somewhere. She walked, then thrashed around the trees.

Let me go home! White Buffalo where are you?

The archway would close if her emotions pulled in both directions. She quieted and looked into her inner light. John pulled the hardest. Their love bound them as one. What if he were already dead and the archway would not open because his energy could not pull her through? What if John's situation was exactly like Mia's? If John was dead and her baby died in 1882, there would be nothing. A few friends, but no joy or purpose. If she returned to 2022, her baby could live. There would be only her husband's child to comfort her in modern society. What if John wasn't dead, and her lack of faith caused him to die? She would never know if she caused his death by not returning. John made a promise to live, and she made a promise to return.

Other things tugged at her heart. Mother Sullivan was becoming the parent she wanted. The homestead with the horses, the unsullied land and water, their cozy cabin, and their marriage bed. Her puppy Billie. These things pulled her to the other side.

What about this baby, so insistent on coming to the world? Sarah believed that her baby had a better chance of living with modern medicine. A new belief, proved by her life in 1882, asserted that the child could receive different care that also would ensure its survival. Maddy's tea gave her instant relief that modern medicine couldn't provide. Coming out of her reverie, Sarah looked at the archway. Still closed. Would she deliver this baby alone, both dying here? Was this chosen path, one that would kill her, John, and their baby?

A strong contraction went through her body. Sarah despaired, "Please help! Somebody, anything, please help me!"

"Mommy?" Sarah froze, "Mommy, why are you crying?"

"Mia, you are here!"

Mia climbed into Sarah's lap like not a day had passed since her death. Mia poked her in her stomach. "You fat, mommy."

Sarah could not help but smile a little. "That's your baby brother or sister."

"A baby?" Mia asked, clearly excited.

"Want to feel the baby?" Sarah held her little hand on the spot where the baby kicked.

"My baby brother."

"Or sister."

"My brother," Mia asserted, in her usual stubborn way. Sarah wondered if Mia was just hard-headed, or if she knew something from her ethereal world.

A hard cramp hit; Sara grimaced, holding her stomach. "Mommy has an owie?" asked Mia in concern. Sarah nodded, still in the throes of the contraction.

"I kiss your owie," Mia leaned down, kissing Sarah on the center of her large baby bump.

Sarah inspected Mia. She was exactly the pre-leukemia three-year-old child. Her hazel eyes still crinkled in a smile. Sarah stroked her blond hair, and still marveled at the little curls. Mia wore the pink sun dress Sarah made her.

"Mia – are you happy?"

Mia shook her head positively. "We are all friends, and we play all of the time."

"Are there any grownups there?"

"We just play."

Sarah wanted to ask if Mia missed her, or if God existed, what happened if you died, should you pray – all topics esoteric and selfish. Her gift from the beyond was Mia, nothing more. As they cuddled by the tree, Sarah became aware of something. Or of the absence of something. Her contractions had been reduced to a dull back ache.

"Mommy's owie better," said Mia, knowingly.

"How did you do that?"

"Kisses make owies better." Mia pulled back, looking at Sarah. "Mommy sad."

"I am. My baby has a new Daddy, and I want to find him."

"He lost?"

"No, he's on the other side of the trees. I can't get there."

Mia thought for a moment. She held Sarah's hand, sliding off her lap. They walked to the trees.

"Is new Daddy here?" There stood the arch, shimmering brightly.

"Oh, Mia, how did you find it?"

Mia said, "I go play now." Her precious child recited:

> *"No monsters in this house,*
>
> *No silly spiders in this house,*
>
> *No bad dreams in this house,*
>
> *Mommy, new Daddy, and baby brother happy in new house."*

Sarah walked through the archway and then looked back. Mia's image glimmered. Sarah threw her a kiss; then her daughter was gone.

John held his end of the bargain. He survived.

"I'm back; I made it!" Sarah leaned down, hugging his hot neck. "I love you so much. It's going to work. You will be up and about, helping me have this baby."

John turned his head back and forth, calling out deliriously." Mustard gas, Bill get the mustard." Then, "Sarah! Come back!"

"I'm back. I brought the medicine. It's going to be OK, sweetie. You still have to try real hard." Sarah expertly inserted the IV needle into his biggest vein. She hung the IV fluids, running them as fast as they would go, using the coat rack as an IV pole. The precious Vancomycin dripped in first, then the other supportive drugs. Using her precious blood pressure cuff, she could barely hear the 72/40 reading.

Mother Sullivan helped Sarah bathed John as gently as she would bathe their baby. She talked all along, not caring what the older woman would hear. "When I got there the archway was closed. I wouldn't let myself be afraid. Finally, I kept thinking about the medicine. I pictured getting it; I pictured bringing it back to you." She wrung out the cloth, rinsing his chest with fresh water. "It worked; I got through!" They changed his sweat-soaked sheets. Sarah kept talking, trying to keep John in this world. "Jane and Joe were shocked to see me of course. Joe rounded up the medicines. Jane bought me a whole new wardrobe. With boots! You know how I hated those old boots."

Sarah accomplished her part; John had to do the rest. She sat in the rocker, holding his hand. Mother Sullivan left the room, keeping a close ear on Sarah's ongoing monolog. "Something terrible happened on the way back. Don't worry, it's OK now. The baby started to come! I tried everything I knew, but I couldn't stop the labor." John's mutterings quieted. "I got to the archway in labor, and I couldn't get through." I was so afraid. I thought we all were going to die. But we were saved. Mia came! Do you hear me? It was Mia! She kissed me and stopped my labor then helped me find my way through. Oh, John, Mia saved all of us." Sarah checked his blood pressure again. 80/60. Something was working. Maybe a little bit of everything was working. She didn't mean to fall asleep in the rocker. The last thing she remembered was murmuring to John, "Mia said the baby is a boy. I wonder if she knows."

At dawn, Sarah woke when the baby kicked her bladder. John! He lay pale, his lips white. For a few interminable seconds, he did not breathe. He then inhaled deeply, and his hands twitched. Oh, my God, he made it through the night. Sarah slipped back into her regular dress. She was grateful Mother Sullivan once again didn't question her strange clothing. Dr. Hancock arrived as she finished dressing.

"How is he?"

"Alive."

The doctor looked at the IV and associated paraphernalia on the coat rack. "The only place things like this can come from is the future. Is that your mysterious archway?"

"It no longer matters; I cannot return to that place. There is no future; there is only now."

He watched her use the blood pressure cuff with amazement. "What is that?"

It measures the strength of the heart when the heart contracts and when it is still. It is a critical medical instrument. Last night, John's blood pressure was 72/40, hardly compatible with life." She pumped the bulb. Slowly the dial released. "It is 96/52. He's getting better." The doctor examined John and stood at the foot of the bed, stroking his mustache. "I don't want to give false hope; he is incrementally better this morning. His pulse is a little lower. His temperature is lower. The leg looks the same."

"All the intravenous fluids I gave him have reversed the dehydration." On this critical day, their large group of friends milled outside the house all over the yard. Every ear strained for updates. Every update was examined for all of its possible meanings for John's survival. Sarah and Dr. Hancock sat with John. Bill and Adele visited briefly. Adele had been crying, and Sarah saw Bill pull her close. Mother Sullivan was the rock of Gibraltar as always. She served the church lady's food, doling it out with concern for everybody. Maddy sat in the living room chair, her presence a calm comfort to all. Mother Sullivan divulged Sarah's difficult trip into Maddy's ear. Maddy started to stand but realized Sarah would not leave John's side.

Noon came without any appreciable change. Sarah's determined mind felt that with the medicine, John could fight and survive. Late in the afternoon, Sarah sat in the kitchen with Adele. Adele had baked luscious cinnamon rolls that smelled so good they even drew Sarah out of the bedroom. Adele kept up her usual chatter. As she sipped her tea, Sarah noticed it was often "Bill this," or Bill said."

"Adele," she interrupted. "Are you and Bill courting?"

Of course, Adele's cheeks flamed. Her usual shyness was absent though. She looked straight at Sarah with a wide grin. "Yes, he is courtin' me. Cain't you imagine a man like Bill likin' me? He knows everything about me even. He says don't judge a person from the past, but from what they are now."

"Bill is fortunate to get a woman as good as you."

Sarah heard noise from the bedroom. A raspy voice called, "Sarah? Sarah? Where is my wife?" Sarah knocked her chair over in her haste to get to John.

"John?"

He struggled to sit, his weak arms giving out. "You made it back."

"And you stayed alive. I gave you the medicine, you are getting better." The pressure of the days cracked open. She fell to her knees next to John. He lifted a shaky hand, stroking her hair.

Sarah did not think that John was a model patient. Or a tolerant patient. Or by definition, patient at all. Sarah didn't mind that he insisted on getting out of bed; it was good for his circulation. What she did mind was finding him swaying precariously when he decided he could do it himself. She ran to steady him, taking the weight of his body on her shoulder. "John! You are going to fall and hurt yourself even more." She sat heavily on the chair. You are going to hurt me and our baby if I have to catch you."

John looked contrite. "I'm sorry, Sarah, it is just so frustrating to feel like I am not a man. I won't do it again."

Sarah began physical therapy as soon as the healing allowed.

"Easy as she goes, girl," gritted John.

"No pain, no gain," sympathized Sarah. She distracted him with more stories of the future.

It took another week before John was ready to stand with Bill on one side and a homemade crutch on the other. His face turned grey with the effort. Anemia from loss of blood slowed his progress. Mrs. Sullivan fed him meat and liver and anything she could think of to boost his blood. John's determination led to three steps, then five. The day he could walk to the porch was a victory. He insisted on sitting outside to breathe in the late fall smells. Progress came in small steps. First the sitting, then the walking on the porch. One week John aimed his wounded leg and crutch and made it to the barn. He was covered with sweat and his good leg quivered. He picked up the scoop and fed Chestnut her morning oats. Proud of this small contribution, he said to Sarah, "I'm back."

Sarah's face shone with sweat. Her beautiful hair hung down her shoulders in wet strands. Another contraction started. "Here we go again," John whispered in her ear. Sarah had been laboring for eight hours now. She thought of all the women who were told to just breathe through their contractions. That's the biggest bullshit line ever fed to women. John was her rock. He held her hand through each wretched contraction. Even his farm-hardened hands ached from the strength of her grip. He wiped the sweat from her forehead and dabbed cool water on her neck. He rubbed her lower back with his fists hard against her spine.

Sarah's anxiety began to rise when she stopped progressing. Maddy said, "Don't fight the contractions girl, ride with them."

"I'm trying! It hurts too much. Why did I think I could do this?"

"Look at all the love in this room helping you," said Mother Sullivan.

Adele, who finally had to be told not to chatter, patted her hand.

"It's gone on too long; I am afraid."

John knew his wife well. He prepared for this moment a few weeks ago. "I think it is time for a limerick"

"Jesus Christ John," she flashed with anger.

My wife is pregnant and how.

She really is big as a cow.

She can't touch her toes,

And waddles as she goes,

I'm ready for the baby right now!

Silence descended. Nobody knew how to take the insulting joke. Sarah paused, not reacting at first. Then absurdity sunk in. She laid her head back into his arms and laughed out loud. "You are terrible!" she giggled. "It is going to take you years to make up for that insult." John's humor worked. Sarah relaxed and began pushing a half hour later. An hour into pushing, Sarah's

277

progression stopped again. John held her from behind, urging her to push, push, push with every contraction. She tried mightily. Maddy encouraged her - "The head is right there, a few more pushes and you will be done." But a few more pushes did not do the job. Every woman in the room involuntarily bore down with each contraction, willing the baby out with their own inner strength. Sarah was tired after two hours. Adele wiped her tears of frustration. Maddy helped her sip a special tea for strength. The energy in the room was tense. Sarah pushed half-heartedly for the next two contractions. John whispered something in her ear. "Not now John. I don't care. I can't push anymore."

John whispered in her ear. "You have the strength. You are the woman who lives in two centuries. You save children and husbands. You not only learned to live in a strange place, but you also made it better. You are the strongest woman, no, strongest person I know. Just a few more tries. Sarah, I want you to look into the innermost light in your heart. You will find that woman there." The familiar words of love and strength gave her the motivation she needed. Sarah gave three more pushes, and their son was born.

Maddy lay the baby on Sarah's chest, waiting a few minutes to cut the cord, The new parents cried the tears that only a new birth evokes. The emotion pierced John's heart and brought him to his knees next to the bed. Mother Sullivan wiped the baby as the new parents wondered at his fingers, his little feet, and his total trust in his new home. Safe and warm, he opened his little eyes for the first time to take in his new world.

'What's his name?" blurted Adele.

Stay or Go?

John looked at Sarah, and she nodded. "Ainsley Davey McIntyre."

"I know Ainsley is your father's name," said Mother Sullivan. Is Davey a family name, too?"

"No," whispered Sarah. "It means beloved.

☐

279

Epilogue

Sarah rummaged through her doctor's bag, readying for a day in town. She couldn't find her blood pressure cuff at first but finally found it in the corner on the floor. A certain child had gotten into her bag.

She needed to be more careful; the cuff was irreplaceable. The second cuff had been presented to Dr. Hancock as payment for his care. He felt awed by this instrument from the future. Sarah spent a day teaching him how to use it and interpret the readings.

She headed to the door to mount Clover. A devoted father almost missed her as he was laughing with the boy on his shoulders. "Don't you kiss your wife goodbye anymore?" Sarah took in her family's happiness with a swelled heart.

"Oops." John kissed her, then bent over so she could kiss her little one.

"We are going fishing mom." Said the four-year-old.

Stay or Go?

"And you can't come," mocked John.

"Why can't I come? I am still part of the family, aren't I?" Sarah played the game.

"Because it's a Boy's Club!" they chorused. John prompted the children, "OK, one, two three, GO!" They all turned to her and stuck out their tongues. Even the little one opened his mouth, hanging out his tongue.

Sarah laughed. "When do I get a Girl's Club?"

John nodded at her expanding belly. "If you ever get that girl you want so bad."

"You promised me a girl last time."

"This time, next time, we'll see."

Sarah watched as her boys laughed, and ran towards the creek. Heart overflowing, she mounted Clover. Adele, due about the same time as Sarah, waved goodbye. Sarah trotted off, her path defined by love.

Made in United States
Troutdale, OR
10/18/2024

23574005R00170